THE CHRISTMAS ARRANGEMENT

A MISTLETOE MOUNTAIN NOVEL

MELISSA F. MILLER

BROWN STREET BOOKS

This one's for families. The ones we inherit and the ones we make— however messy and imperfect they may be.

PLAYLIST

Here's music to set the mood while you read *The Christmas Arrangement*. Add a cozy corner and your favorite beverage! You can also find the playlist on my website, melissafmiller.com.

"Glittery," Kacey Musgraves, Troye Sivan
"Officially Christmas," Dan + Shay
"Too Sweet," Hozier
"Last Christmas," Clementine Duo
"Sweet December," Brett Eldredge, Kelly Clarkson
"Opalite," Taylor Swift
"The Cozy Song," Dan + Shay
"Make It to Christmas," Alessia Cara
"Wish List," Colin & Caroline
"Santa Will Find You," Mindy Smith
"Winter Song," Leslie Odom, Jr., Cyntia Erivo
"Something about December," Christina Perri

"Love Is Christmas," Sara Bareilles

"Christmas Tree Farm," Taylor Swift

"Merry Christmas, Darling," Christina Perri

"Foxes in the Snow,"Jason Isbell

"If You Love Her," Forest Blakk

"Ivy," Taylor Swift

"Stay with Me," Emma Steinbakken

"Under the Tree," Ed Sheeran

"Bloom," The Paper Kites

"Honey," Taylor Swift

"Maybe this Christmas," Michael Bublé, Carly Pearce

"Present Without a Bow," Kacey Musgraves, Leon Bridges

"Beautiful Things," Benson Boone

"Santa Doesn't Know You Like I Do," Sabrina Carpenter

"Single Bells," Lee Brice

"Ceilings," Lizzie McAlpine

"Christmas Lights," Coldplay

"Tis the Season," SAYGRACE

"Holiday Made for Two," David Barnes

"Enough for Me," Jordi

"Only When It Snows," Nova Miller

"If We Were Vampires," Noah Kahan, Wesley Schultz

"Wi$h Li$t," Taylor Swift

"Wonderful Time of Year," Jeremy Lister

"Christmas Tonight," Dave Barnes, Hillary Scott

"Nothing Like You," Dave Barnes

CHAPTER 1

RESCUING A SPIDER

Ivy

A bead of sweat trickles down the back of my neck and runs along my spine to collect in my panties, followed by another, and another. It's unbelievable that I'm sweating like this in late November in Vermont. It's twenty degrees and snowing.

But the MacIntoshes' barn is both heated and packed with photojournalists, entertainment reporters, and camera crews. Between the radiant heat system, the body heat of the crowd, and the heat being thrown by the blindingly bright photography lights trained directly on me, I'm roasting in the sage green wool sweater dress I wriggled into just minutes ago. The dress is soft and weather appropriate, but the thigh-high stiletto boots the stylist paired with it are highly impractical for a snowy day in the mountains. I can only imagine that my carefully coiffed curls are wilting as badly as the flowers are. I eye the drooping scarlet amaryllis and my heart aches. I spent hours arranging literally thousands of blooms into a festive fairy-tale garden. And for what?

None of this is real.

The scene is as fake as it is hot. Speaking of fake and hot, I shift my attention from my poor flower arrangements to the man standing beside me. He holds my clammy left hand loosely in his warm, strong right hand like it's the most natural thing in the world. It most certainly is not the most natural thing in the world for Dash Pine, Sexiest Man Alive, top-grossing movie star, former teen icon, and Hollywood bad boy to be bothering with a small-town florist whose name sounds like something out of a bad Christmas cartoon. Yet, here we are.

He catches my eye and flashes me a reassuring smile. Then he gives my hand a little squeeze and whispers, "Show time."

Quinn flicks the lights off and on like intermission at the ballet is about to end, and the noisy barn goes quiet.

Dash's grin broadens and he greets the assembled media in a friendly, familiar tone, like he's sitting around a fire pit with his buddies. Does Dash Pine have buddies? Has he ever leaned back in a camp chair, propped his feet up on a log, and sipped beer from a can? I have no clue.

"Thanks for coming, folks. I know Mistletoe Mountain

is a trek for most of you, and I'm grateful you made the trip because I have exciting news to share."

He pauses while camera bulbs flash. I curve my glossed lips into a happy smile, trying to think cold thoughts about icicles and snowballs rather than more troubling thoughts like whether the lipliner is bleeding into the foundation that is almost certainly melting off my face.

"Everyone, now that our secret's out, meet Ivy Jolly."

He wraps his arm possessively around my shoulder and tugs me toward him, nestling me into his side. He smells like juniper and cinnamon and man.

"How long have you been together?" A reporter with gorgeous box braids calls out. I recognize her as Veronica Jones from *The New Newz*.

"Long enough that I couldn't wait another minute to share it with the world," he rumbles in his famous throaty voice.

"Ivy, what do you do?"

"I'm a—" My voice comes out in a squeak, so I stop, clear my throat, and breathe before trying again. "I'm a florist. I own Blooms by Ivy in town."

Dash sweeps his free hand expansively over the garden I've created in the dead of winter. "All of this is her work."

My panic ebbs and my pride swells as the cameras and recorders pan over the floral display.

"Dash, how did you two meet?" someone shouts from the middle of the crowd.

I wait for him to field this question. The pause drags on. And then on some more. I flutter my mascara-coated eyelashes and give my supposed boyfriend a look that says, *honey, tell these nice people how we met.*

He's wide-eyed, frozen like a deer on the side of the road that's just heard the roar of a pickup truck. He squeezes my hand again, but this time his palm is as damp as mine is. His Adam's apple bobs above his collar and he blinks rapidly. Dash Pine, trained actor, is choking.

For a heartbeat, I think well, that's it. This ridiculous plan is about to fall apart like the house of cards it is. But here's the thing about me. I can't bear to see anyone—or anything—suffer. Just this morning, I pulled over on the shoulder of the road to relocate a spider from my side mirror to a stand of still-flowering witch hazel trees, nestling the little thing into the yarn-like petals of one reddish-yellow bloom to shelter it from the wind. I can't very well rescue an arachnid and then let a fellow human die a slow death of public humiliation, can I?

"Can I tell the story?" I coo at Dash. My voice sounds sweet and light—a minor miracle considering that my legs are shaking and the rivulets of sweat pooling in my panties have ticked up from droplets to a steady drizzle.

"Please," he croaks.

Several dozen pairs of eyes train on me. I look over the reporters' heads and catch Quinn's gaze. I hold it, talking directly to my best friend, as I spin a tale that's technically entirely true.

"We met on the set of a photo shoot. I was delivering flowers and Dash was outside getting some air. He helped me move a heavy potted plant, and I told him how much I loved his performance in *An Inheritance of Irony*." I pause and giggle. "Maybe it went beyond telling him. I may have gushed a little—okay, a lot." My face heats, and for once, I'm not upset that I blush so easily because several of the cynical Hollywood insiders soften, their skeptical frowns loosening into small smiles.

My intervention reset Dash's brain, and he smoothly jumps in with his famous half-purr, half growl. "We started talking movies, then Ivy told me all about the charming little town she lived in, and I decided I had to see it for myself. We've been more or less inseparable ever since."

While this is also technically true, I steel myself for someone to ask exactly how long we've been a couple. *Three hours* doesn't seem like a good answer.

Turns out, I'm worried for nothing. There's another barrage of flashes as he places his mouth on my ear.

"Thank you." His whisper is a rumble in my chest bone.

I let out a long, shaky breath of relief. How did I get myself into this?

CHAPTER 2

DASH SHOWS HIS ASS. AGAIN.

Dash
Three Hours Earlier

The makeup artist takes in the evidence of last night's debauchery as she turns my face from side to side, inspecting the bags under my eyes and my dehydrated skin.

While Luna mutters in disgust, I listen through the speakerphone to my manager Brody snort like the bull he is. "What is wrong with you?"

Even through the tinny speaker I can tell he's biting the words out from between clenched teeth. Luna's pierced right eyebrow jumps up at his tone.

"What's wrong with *me*? I'm here in the frozen hinterlands. Where's *she*?"

She's the one he should be pissed at. Lia Campbell, America's sweetheart, and the star of the upcoming Christmas rom-com *Sugar Cookies and Spice* was supposed to be here over an hour ago.

"She's not coming."

Disbelief lands like a punch to my sternum. "Not coming? Why not?"

"You can't be surprised. Not after the stunt you pulled last night." His anger gives way to a flatter emotion—resignation, maybe.

I scroll through my fuzzy, fragmented memories. Did I get into another bar fight? Swear at the paparazzi crowded around the club's velvet rope? After a moment, I give up. It's all a blur. A blinding, boozy blur.

Whatever the problem is, it's his problem to manage. It's right there in the name. He's my manager.

I raise my chin, indignant. "Enlighten me anyway."

"Don't move," Luna instructs, waving the concealer wand in warning.

I hold still so she can work her magic and watch the image of Brody on the video call drag one hand through his hair, leaving dozens of spikes in its wake.

"Lia's out. Her agent took me out to breakfast to tell me in person."

"She can't be out. The whole point of me coming to Poinsettia Peak—"

"Mistletoe Mountain," Luna and Brody correct me in unison.

"Wherever. You said I had to do this to redeem myself.

You said a feel-good holiday photo spread, a whirlwind romance with America's sweetheart—"

He cuts me off, pointing a finger at me through the screen. "I know what I said. And I'll remind you that the entire team—your agent, the publicist, the studio, everybody—agreed that this is the right move, possibly the only move that might salvage your career."

My indignation leaks out, my anger deflating like a balloon. "So what happened? I thought she was on board."

"She *was* on board. Her holiday rom-com opened in previews yesterday. A whirlwind romance with a reformed rogue would polish your image *and* give her image a bit of spice while she promotes *Sugar Cookies and Spice*."

"Then what's the problem?"

He sighs deeply and speaks to me in a voice that I imagine a disappointed father would use. I don't know firsthand, having grown up with no father, disappointed or otherwise. But the heavy tone makes me think of a dad imparting wisdom and a life lesson to a wayward son.

"Well, Dash, you went on 'Mornings with Molly' and unleashed a tirade about—"

"Your ass," Luna supplies.

"Remember that?"

"Of course I remember," I sputter. "That's why I'm doing this. For my redemption arc."

This whole mess is the height of irony, which itself is pretty ironic. The reason I filmed *An Inheritance of Irony* in the first place was to revamp my reputation. After a solid decade as a child star on a series of forgettable sit-coms and one dramedy that will haunt me forever, like an undead bloodsucker, I wanted to shake off the mantle of Vlad, the vampire heartthrob, and sink my metaphorical fangs into meatier roles.

An Inheritance of Irony, a serious work of cinema, was supposed to make the public forget about my teenage stunts, ill-advised shenanigans, and thoughtless social media posts. And I'm not being vain when I say I did my best work ever as Cody, the orphaned ranch hand forced to relocate to Philadelphia, where he takes a job caring for a dying art forger. Critics called my portrayal "thoughtful, complex, and layered" and predicted I'd end up with a glittery statuette. I even moved from Los Angeles to New York and had my agent spread the word that I was interested in doing stage work.

But when I hit the PR circuit, all anybody wanted to talk about was my butt.

So, yes, fine, I didn't handle it with a lot of grace when Molly asked how I felt about the nude scenes with a thick layer of innuendo. It didn't help that my naked posterior was plastered on the screen behind the couch while the opening bars of a striptease song blared.

An Inheritance of Irony, far from changing my image to one of a respected thespian, seemed to cement my reputation as an empty-headed himbo. Like I said, ironic.

"A drunken tirade about your ass," Brody clarifies.

"I wasn't drunk," I say weakly.

My manager and makeup artist exchange amused glances through my phone.

He snorts. "Did you forget we were in the green room with you?"

"Nobody gets drunk on a Bloody Mary."

"Maybe not. But how about seven Bloody Marys?" Luna retorts.

"I hadn't had breakfast," I mumble. Then the burn of humiliation eases as righteous anger takes over. "Lia knew all this when she agreed. She has no right to back out now."

"She wouldn't have. But then you went clubbing in Brooklyn last night."

"So?"

He exhales, flaring his nostrils. "So, when you stumbled out of one of the many nightclubs you visited, the photographer for *Tinseltown Tattler* called you Bubble Booty."

I squint, as I try and fail to remember. Finally, I shake my head, lost.

He wastes no time filling me in. "In response, you turned around, dropped your jeans, and bared the booty in question right there in the middle of the sidewalk. I can't believe you don't remember mooning the press."

I did *what?* My cheeks flame.

"How many Bloody Marys did you have last night?" Luna snickers.

I ignore her and cover my embarrassment by turning on Brody. "Fixing things is your job. Fix it."

"I can't fix it, Dash. Your naked butt is all over the internet now. Lia's not coming. Her creative team is telling her it's a bad idea. Frankly, they're right. She shouldn't tie herself to you. That's what I'd tell her if she were my client."

His disapproval stings. A lot. He's been my manager since I was twelve. He's like an uncle to me, but that doesn't change the facts: he works for me. "Well, she's not your client. I am."

He's silent for a long moment.

"And as your manager, I'm telling you you're screwed."

The words leave me reeling like a right hook to the jaw. Five years of clawing my way up the greased pole of respectability. Five years of fighting to be taken seriously. And finally, right as I reach the top, I slide right back into the pit of disposable, interchangeable pretty boys where I started.

No, this is even worse. At least teenaged Dash was too stupid to know he was a punch line.

I blink at him. "That's it? I'm screwed?"

"That's it. Unless a miracle falls into our laps."

Before I can tear him a new one, thanks to the magic of cellular data, the call drops. I stare at the blank screen in disbelief.

Luna chuckles. "The coverage here sucks, but Brody's timing, as always, is impeccable."

I don't laugh. "What am I gonna do?"

"Pray for a Christmas miracle."

I spring from the chair and storm out of the room. I need some air.

CHAPTER 3

WINTER WONDERLAND: CELEBRITY EDITION

Ivy
Three hours earlier

I'm wrestling with a large white snowball hydrangea when a high-pitched shriek sounds directly behind me. I jump and nearly drop the heavy planter on my foot. I bobble it and, at the last second, ease it into the red wagon I borrowed from my dad along with his red pickup truck.

The wagon's nearly full of blooms, but I've barely made a dent in the mountain of flowers still in the truck bed. I really should've wrangled someone into helping me with this delivery. Preferably someone muscular.

I brush the thought away. I am woman, hear me roar. Or grunt, at least. Thankfully, I don't have to traverse the frozen, rocky ground with all these flowers. As requested, the wide doors to the MacIntoshes' heated barn were propped open for me so I could back the pickup into the space, protecting the flowers from the elements.

I push my bangs out of my eyes and tuck them back under the hood of my parka as I turn in the direction of the nails-on-a-chalkboard noise. As suspected, it's coming from Quinn MacIntosh. Her curly blonde hair bounces, probably from the decibel level.

Correction: the bouncing curls are courtesy of the way her entire body is jittering and twitching as she crosses the threshold from the blustery outdoors into the barn.

"Where have you *been?*" Against all odds, her voice climbs even higher up the vocal register.

I flash her a slight frown as I resume the task of hauling oversized flower arrangements out of the truck bed and nestling them in the wagon.

Quinn and my sisters and I have been friends since she and I were both in diapers. Holly, Merry, and I call her dads Uncle Chris and Uncle Pedro. She calls our father Papa Nick. It's that kind of friendship. In all this time, I've never known her to be high strung.

"I've been at the shop putting together your order." I speak in a soothing tone like she's a rabid raccoon. "And, I'm *early.* Why are you tweaking? Did Merry stop by with a plate of her chocolate-espresso balls?"

I *told* my sister to cut back on the espresso powder in her eleventh-hour energy bites, but she insisted people need the boost to get through the jam-packed month of

December festivities that Mistletoe Mountain is famous for. She has a point, but poor Quinn looks like she's about to blast off.

"What? No." Her eyes grow huge. "She's not coming out here, is she? She can't!"

She's as edgy as a reindeer on an ice-slicked roof. I make the universal gesture for 'calm down' with my mittened hands. "She didn't say anything about a surprise visit. It was just a guess based on how amped up you are. What's going on with you?"

She heaves a long, loud sigh of relief and ignores the question. "Oh, good. I don't need another lecture about the NDA."

I pause with a brilliant red amaryllis in my arms and raise an eyebrow. "NDA? As in a nondisclosure agreement?"

She nods.

"What kind of photo shoot is this, anyway?"

"I told you—it's a really big deal."

To be fair, she did. In fact, she said it at least three or four times. But I figured she just wanted me to squeeze her enormous, last-minute order into my already over-scheduled holiday season calendar.

I've known since before the jack-o-lantern smashing contest in early November that I'd bit off more than I could chew in my first year as Mistletoe Mountain's only local florist. And, yikes, was I right.

Mind you, I'm not complaining. Opening Blooms by Ivy back in August was a leap of faith that stretched my budget until it was paper-thin. Except for Sunday dinners at the inn with my dad and Noelle and the meals that my sisters have treated me to, it's been four long months of rice and beans on repeat. But, come New Year's day, I'll be in the black.

A large part of my pending financial stability is thanks to Quinn. And not just because of this massive order, either. She opened Quintessentially Quinn, her event planning business, less than a month before I signed the lease on the flower shop. She finally took everyone's advice and turned MacIntosh Farm's gorgeous old barn into a full-time event venue. And as soon I opened my doors, we partnered to offer package deals for her space and my flowers.

We were slammed with weddings and graduation parties, anniversary parties, and family reunions all summer, then she rolled right into engagement parties and family photo shoots all autumn and I started ramping up for the bajillion holiday parties, open houses, events, and traditions that dominate town from the day after Thanksgiving through December 31st.

So when she called me just two days ago with a last-minute floral emergency (her words), of course I agreed to help her out, despite the fact that I'm completely booked and the Christmas festivities kick-off tonight.

The so-called emergency? She needs *one thousand* blooming flowers along with greenery and berries to create "an elegant, magical, romantic winter wonderland with a touch of small-town whimsy."

After I made her repeat herself, I did some quick calculations and told her I'd have to import at least half of the flowers, which would make the sky-high cost even more outrageous.

Her response? *The client said you have a blank check.*

So, thirty-seven hours (and one all-nighter) later, here we are. I've loaded my dad's borrowed pickup with red, cream, and champagne roses, ivy, holly, deep red peonies, and fragrant Christmas lilies, giant amaryllis, bright red dinner plate hibiscus, and several more varieties that I'm forgetting in the haze of exhaustion and exhilaration.

I've been so busy making this order happen, I haven't stopped to wonder who would want such an extravagant display, let alone why.

Now, I squint at Quinn. "Are Taylor and Travis getting married in your barn?"

She giggles. "I wish, but no. You aren't that far off, though."

My narrowed eyes widen. "Seriously?"

"Seriously. And I can tell you who it is as soon as you sign this."

She digs into her parka pocket, removes a folded sheet of paper and a pen, and thrusts them at me.

I unfold the paper and smooth it out, then give it a quick scan and raise an eyebrow. "You want me to sign an NDA, too? Just to deliver the flowers?"

She shrugs. "The client's insisting—or at least his manager is."

I skim the rest of the single-spaced document and almost uncap the pen. Then I freeze. My oldest sister would throw a legendary lawyerly fit if I signed this thing without understanding it.

"I need to show this to Holly first."

She shakes her head. "There's no time. Besides, isn't she in Florida?"

Holly spent Thanksgiving with her boyfriend's family. But she and Jack are on their way back to Vermont right now because he wouldn't miss the town Christmas tree lighting for love or money. He considers it their first date. She begs to differ.

She *always* begs to differ. Like I said, she's a lawyer. She was born to argue.

Now I glance from the document in my hand to Quinn then back to the contract. "She'll be back tonight."

"Look. I promise it's okay to sign it. I signed the same thing. My dad looked it over and said it was completely standard."

Presuming she means her dad the judge and not her dad the artist, that's comforting. But still. I don't want to do something that gets my fledgling little business in trouble.

I gnaw at my lower lip, trying to decide.

Quinn, sensing weakness, moves in for the kill. "And so did your dad and Noelle. I'm sure Holly reviewed it for them."

I jerk my head up. "They did?"

"Yep. This same client rented the cottage at your dad's inn for the week."

I squint at her, skeptical. "There's no way. Jodi and Mark Bryant reserve it every year."

"They didn't last year," she reminds me.

"That was a one-time thing," I protest weakly.

She shrugs. "Guess it's a two-time thing now. You can ask your dad when you return his truck. Just sign the thing already, please."

The pleading tone in her voice melts my resistance and I scribble my name on the signature line. She plucks the document out of my hand and spins around like she's going to leave in a hurry.

"Wait. You have to tell me who the client is. You said you couldn't tell me until I signed. I signed, so spill it."

She stops and turns around to face me. "Dash Pine."

My jaw drops. "Dash Pine as in Dash Pine?"

"I don't know how to answer that question. Dash Pine as in the guy who played Vlad Graves on *The Vampire Quarterback* for the entirety of our teenage years."

I stammer out some sounds that mean nothing. My ability to form words appears to be broken.

But Quinn correctly guesses I'm trying to ask what Dash Pine is doing in Mistletoe Mountain, and why it requires a metric buttload of fresh flowers.

"He's dating Lia Campbell. It must be getting serious. They've decided to go public with their relationship right here in our holiday hamlet." She flashes a wide grin.

"Dash Pine and Lia Campbell?" I manage to ask.

"Yep, Hollywood's bad boy and America's sweetheart

are in love. They want to take advantage of the golden hour for the photo shoot. Please work your winter wonderland magic as fast as you can. Trust me, you do *not* want to get on their bad side. I gotta go. Sorry I can't help you unload."

I barely hear her over the teenage version of me freaking out inside my brain. *Dash Pine.* **The** *Dash Pine.* The broody vampire quarterback who stared down at me from the poster above my bed from 2012 through 2017, inclusive.

I hush my inner sixteen-year-old. Meeting Dash Pine may be teenaged Ivy's wildest dream come true, but I'm an adult. A business owner. A woman who would like to eventually be able to buy groceries without counting her quarters first.

I can't afford to act like a starstruck fangirl. This contract's too important. If the photos of Dash and Lia go viral, every bride between Maine and Rhode Island will be at my door.

Holy sugarplums.

CHAPTER 4

PLAN B

Dash
Two hours and forty minutes earlier

I can't believe Lia is screwing me over like this. She'll get hers, though. I've been in the business long enough to know that, at some point, her sweet facade will slip, and she'll need an image makeover of her own. When karma catches up to her, I'll take plenty of satisfaction in it. But at the moment, Brody's right. I'm screwed.

And whose fault is that? Lia didn't moon the press. Lia didn't get hammered on a morning show.

I should be pissed off at myself, not her. I'm the jackhole here.

The cold wind swirling down the collar of my leather

coat does nothing to cool off my rising temper. I pull my beanie down over my brow and storm away from the house toward the event barn, walking fast in an effort to burn off some of my anger. I'm maybe forty yards from the barn when I hear the grunting. Like a gym bro lifting four hundred pounds grunting. A vet carrying a cow grunting. Big, manly, grunting.

Curious, I round the corner in search of the source. Based on the sound effects, the smart money is on a farmer facing down a black bear. So imagine my surprise when I spot a woman wrestling a flower pot out of the bed of a pickup truck.

To be fair, it's an enormous planter. She can barely wrap her arms around it. But again, flowers. Not an apex predator or a pregnant cow. A gigantic riot of creamy white and deep red blooms.

"Son of a reindeer," she mutters fiercely.

I snort, and she turns her head to the side to eye me over her shoulder.

"Oh, hi. Could you lend me a hand?"

I don't know the last time someone asked me for a favor. I look at her for a few seconds, as she bobbles the planter. She lowers her chin and stares at me, like she can't believe I'm just standing there watching her struggle.

I snap out of it and jog toward her. "Sure, here."

I ease the heavy pot out of her hands and she immediately grabs another, slightly smaller urn from the truck bed.

"Thanks. This way."

She heads into the barn without another glance at me. It occurs to me that she has no idea who I am. This fact is oddly exciting. For at least a few minutes, I don't have to be The Dash Pine. I can just be me. I trail her inside and catch my breath.

When Brody suggested this place for the big reveal of my fake romance, I had some doubts. More like, I thought he'd mixed up his gummies with the candy ones again. But I have to hand it to Quinn, the barn hits all the right notes. Globe lights drip from the rafters and fresh greenery curls around the supports. And there are flowers everywhere. I mean, everywhere.

I recognize roses, but that's about it. I don't know what the rest of these are but it's like something out of a storybook.

"Wow."

I don't realize I've said it aloud until the woman sets down the planter in her hand and turns to grin at me. "Right?"

Before I can respond, her green eyes go huge and her cheeks, already pink from the cold, turn bright red.

She gapes at me, then closes her eyes and mutters to herself, "Way to press Dash flipping Pine into manual labor, Ivy."

The anonymity was nice while it lasted. But this pot is heavy, so I cut her freakout short. "Ivy, is it? Where do you want this thing?"

She snaps her eyes open and scurries toward me. "Here, give it to me. I'm so sorry, Mr. Pine. I didn't—"

"—I carried a horse in my last film. I can carry a plant. Where should I put it?"

She gestures to a spot next to an equally enormous arrangement that she must've muscled inside by herself. I squat to lower the planter into position, wondering if she lifts weights.

By the time I straighten to standing, her stricken expression gives way to a knowing grin.

"Thank you."

"My pleasure, Ivy. It *is* Ivy, right?"

"Yes. Ivy Jolly, of Blooms by Ivy."

I can't help it, I cackle. "Ivy Jolly? Come on. That's not your real name."

She heaves a sigh and says in a bored tone, "Yes, it is. I'm one of the Jolly sisters—Holly, Ivy, and Merry. And whatever joke you're about to make, I assure you, I've heard it before."

"Those are some"—I pause to search for the least offensive descriptor—"festive names."

Her grin returns with an impish twist. "You should know. "Isn't Dash short for *Dasher*? As in the reindeer? And not to be a pedant, but in the movie, wasn't it a newborn foal? And you didn't really *carry* it so much as lift it briefly. Right?"

It's a surprising show of spirit for this small-town florist to bust my balls. But, truth be told, I like it. "Both fair points. In fact, want to know a secret?"

She nods.

I lower my voice and lean close to her. "They wouldn't let me hold the real foal. It was a fifty-pound bag of flour and post-production special effects."

It's her turn to laugh. And, man, her laugh is a languid, mellifluous sound, like sweet honey flowing. I want to pour it over me. As soon as I have the thought, I shake my head—where did *that* image come from?

Oblivious to my deranged musings, she says, "Well, you were great in that movie even if it was a bag of flour that you rescued from the flood."

"You saw the movie?"

She blinks. "Sure."

I steel myself, waiting for the obligatory comment about my butt.

Instead she says, "I loved it. You gave a raw and vulnerable performance."

"You thought my performance was raw and vulnerable?" I can't keep the satisfaction out of my voice as I repeat her words.

She throws me a questioning look. "Didn't I just say that?"

"Actors," I tell her. "We're needy."

She smiles again, a wide, genuine smile that crinkles her eyes. " You were fantastic. I believed you as Cody Jones." The smile falters. "I'm sorry everyone seems to be focusing on your ass ... ets instead of your artistry."

The tightness that's been a constant in my chest since the disastrous interview loosens. When was the last time someone looked at me and saw anything other than Bubble Booty or Vlad the Vampire QB? It's been years. The next thought that pops into my head is wild, but I say it anyway.

"Would you take off your coat?" I gesture at the puffy white parka that covers her from head to mid-calf.

Her face, framed by the white faux fur that trims her hood, setting off those big green eyes and cold-pinked cheeks splashed with freckles, turns an even deeper red as she blushes furiously.

She furrows her brow. "Take it off?"

"Please." I smile reassuringly, and, I hope, sanely.

She manages a very small, very uncertain return smile.

I'm moderately surprised to find myself holding my breath while I wait for her to decide.

After an interminable moment, she pushes her hood down from her head to reveal a mass of long strawberry blonde hair pinned up on the top of her head in a braided knot. Then she unzips the heavy coat and wriggles out of it. It pools on the wood planks at her feet.

I exhale and study her. She's nothing like the gorgeous, glamorous Lia Campbell. But, she's pretty. No. Not pretty, lovely. It's not a word in my regular vocabulary. But it's what pops to mind. Ivy Jolly is lovely.

She's slight and fair. And with her light red hair and bright green eyes she's my physical opposite. A striking contrast to my olive skin, jet black hair, dark eyes, and a hard-earned muscular frame. A romance between me and a small-town florist might hold even more appeal for my public than would one between me and a fellow movie star —even Lia.

The more I think about it, the better it seems. This could work. And, unlike the lifeless business arrangement Lia and I negotiated through our managers, it already feels strangely real.

"I'd like to date you," I blurt.

CHAPTER 5

REDDER THAN RUDOLPH'S NOSE

Ivy
Two and half hours earlier

"Date me?" I repeat, certain I've misheard.

My nervous system is going haywire at the moment. I mean, I made a movie star carry a planter, insulted his name and his physical prowess, and taken off my coat at his request. I'm blushing like it's my job, my heart is flip-flopping in my chest, and I can't stop staring at him. The thick, black hair, the liquid brown eyes, the chiseled cheekbones. Dash Pine, in the flesh, is standing less than three feet away from me. There's an excellent chance he said something else.

I study him closer, noting the dark smudges under his

famous eyes and a distinct greenish pallor. Maybe he said *I have the flu.*

I instinctively step back. The last thing I need is to get sick during the holiday season.

But he says, "Yes. Will you date me?"

He's studying me back with a spark of … something … in his warm brown eyes. I force myself to hold his gaze levelly and pretend not to notice the heat creeping up my neck to my cheeks under his scrutiny.

As a ghostly pale redhead and a certified shy person, *everything* makes me flush. So it's not exactly surprising that I've been blushing nonstop under the sustained attention of one of the most gorgeous, most famous men on the planet. Unbidden, the image of his bare butt pops into my mind in all its naked glory, and my skin blazes.

What's redder than Rudolph's nose? That's gotta be my face right now.

Part of me wants to flee the barn, jump in the truck, and drive back to town. But most of me is wildly curious. And that part wins.

"I don't understand. Are you asking me out? Aren't you here to announce your relationship with Lia Campbell?"

"There's been a development."

"What kind of development?"

"She's not coming. So there's not going to be an announcement."

The low timbre of his voice, somewhere between a purr and a growl, pins me to the spot even as the words register and my excitement at breathing the same air as Dash Pine dissipates.

"What about all this?" I gesture around the barn.

If I have to eat the cost of all these blooms, I'll be pinching pennies until the Fourth of July. Probably longer. Panic sends my brain into overdrive. Ideas to sell the flowers and recover some of my money tumble around in my brain, colliding into each other and bouncing off my skull: I can set up a flower cart at the tree lighting; partner with Merry for a dessert and flower arrangement special; partner with Holly for a bail hearing and flower arrangement special; or drive around to the funeral homes in the valley and hawk flowers to mourners. Something.

He's still watching me, so I try to arrange my expression into something other than abject horror. But my facial muscles are numb, like I've had a shot of novocaine. Actually, I'm tingly all over.

I must be having an out-of-body experience. Or I'm in shock at the prospect of having to load a thousand-plus flowers back into the pickup truck and figure out what to do with them. Yeah, that's probably it. Shock.

Then Dash says in that same growly voice, "Unless you agree to date me."

"What?" Even in a single syllable my bafflement comes through loud and clear.

"Only for a week. Just when the cameras are around."

"Pretend to date you, you mean?"

"Sure, you could put it that way."

"No, thank you," I say as politely as I can.

He throws me an incredulous look. "You're joking."

"I'm not," I assure him.

"I don't understand the problem."

"You don't? Then maybe I don't understand what you're proposing. I thought I heard you say you want me to pose as your girlfriend. Do I have that wrong?"

"No, you've got it right. Glad we could clear that up." He turns up the wattage on his smile, momentarily distracting me with his impossibly white teeth.

When I gather my wits, I narrow my eyes. "Hard pass."

"Why?"

"Um, maybe because you're dating Lia Campbell. You came here to announce your relationship to the world, but she can't make it. So you're breaking up with her? I'm not about to get caught up in that mess."

He frowns. "I'm not sure if you've heard, but I've had some recent less-than-favorable publicity."

"Bootygate?" I deadpan.

He groans. "You have heard."

"I don't know exactly how quaint you think this town is, but we *do* have the internet."

"Then you know how important it is for me to change the narrative. A sweet holiday romance with someone like you will push that mess of the front page and, more importantly, off the For You Page."

I stare at him as realization dawns. I wonder if a cartoon lightbulb is blinking above my head.

"Ahhh, I get it. Not a romance with *me*. A romance with *someone like me*. Someone fresh-faced and scandal-free.

Someone who could stand in for the star of *Sugar and Spice* because she probably finds you too toxic to even fake date."

His jaw flexes but he dips his head in acknowledgment. "You've nailed it. Lia's team agreed to a public relationship with me for business reasons. But after yesterday, they think it would be a bad idea."

"So, it would be bad PR for Lia, but I should do it anyway. Why?"

"You're not promoting a Christmas rom-com movie."

I counter, "But I am running a business. And this is the busiest season for, well, everyone in town. I can't step away for a week to rehab some actor's image even if I wanted to —which, to be clear, I don't."

"You really don't want to spend a week with someone who's been voted one of the sexiest men alive four years running?" His tone oozes disbelief. "Is this because I mooned the photographers? I don't usually do that, I promise."

His reaction should come across as arrogance, but it doesn't. He simply knows who he is.

And I know who I am, which is why I do not want to be his pretend girlfriend.

"Look. I'm really shy. I don't love the spotlight. My family calls me the only quiet Jolly. And let's not forget, I'm a florist, not an actor. I wouldn't be convincing."

He flicks my extremely valid objections away with the back of his hand. "I'll be convincing enough for both of us."

"I'm flattered. Really. But I have a business to run."

"No problem. I'll pay to bring in a team to take care of your shop."

He says this like it's a done deal, but my back goes up and I bristle. If I were a porcupine, he'd look like a pin cushion right now.

"Absolutely not," I huff.

"Why not?"

"My clients expect—and are entitled to—my personal involvement. I really care about my work." I pause to think of a good metaphor to explain this. "Would you have agreed to a stand-in for the nude scenes in *An Inheritance of Irony?*"

"Would've solved a lot of problems," he grumbles.

I jut out a hip and pin him with a long look until he caves.

"Of course not. It would have been inauthentic."

"Right. And bringing in a team of people who don't know me, my business, or my customers would be equally inauthentic. Besides, there must be a dozen women in town who would jump at the chance to be your girlfriend for the week."

"I don't want them. I want you." He says it bluntly and without hesitation.

"Why?"

"You actually watched the movie. Not for the memes, not to leer at me. You cared about the story."

I feel myself softening, and I *almost* give in. But the reality is I genuinely can't afford to. I use a gentle tone when I say, "I wish I could help you, Dash. But I really don't have time. I'm buried under an avalanche of flower orders.

"I'll help you," he says, breathless.

"You'll help me? You mean, with the orders?"

"Yes. It's a great idea. That's what a real boyfriend would do, right?"

I suppose it *is* what a real boyfriend would do. But to be honest, I can't see him clipping the thorns off roses and arranging greenery.

He must sense my skepticism because he continues, "I can do it. If you'll let me. Didn't I carry that planter like a champ?" He points to the garden roses and peonies with naked pride.

I can't help but laugh. "What would this involve, exactly?"

"Not much, really. You'll stand beside me when I tell the press we're dating. Then I'll take questions and we'll pose for pictures. After that, I'll ask them to respect our privacy while we spend a week together. There's nothing that gets you a more sustained media focus than asking for privacy. So, they'll follow us around to get candid footage of us … uh, doing traditional quaint and picturesque Christmas … things. And I'll pitch in as a flower delivery guy or whatever you need."

"Do you have any favorite holiday traditions?" I have to ask because he seems so unsure of what we would be doing.

He shrugs, and it feels defensive. "Not really. It was just me and mom growing up, and I was usually working. So we'd celebrate wherever I was filming. It was different every year."

My heart squeezes. I can't imagine a childhood without holiday traditions. Shoot, I can't imagine an *adulthood* without them. A highlight reel of decorating trees, baking cookies, filling stockings, and dancing with the rest of the candies in the Land of the Sweets loops through my mind.

Misinterpreting my silence, he tries another tack. "Being known as Dash Pine's girlfriend, even briefly, will be marketing fairy dust for your business."

I waver, but not because of the potential business upside. If I do this, I could take him to the tree lighting, Christmas karaoke, the library book bingo, the ginger-bread house contest, and a dozen other events. I could make up for a lifetime of quiet Christmases past for Dash.

Holly would tell me to run away. Merry would tell me to run into his arms.

I've spent my whole life being the sister who listens. I wonder what it will be like to be the one who's seen. I shiver with an unexpected zing of excitement (or maybe it's nerves).

I extend my right hand.

He stares at it.

"You'll do it?"

"Traditionally, a handshake signifies a deal, Dash."

He ignores my outstretched hand and swoops me into a hug, picking me up and spinning me around.

CHAPTER 6

A HARD TRUTH

Dash
Back to the present

Does my mouth linger a fraction of a second too long on Ivy's ear? Maybe. Does her skin smell like vanilla and roses? Definitely. Did she just save my million-dollar ass with her quick thinking? Clearly.

I should have been prepared for the question of how we met. It was an obvious one and not having a ready answer was sloppy. I know this, but the point's driven home by the way Luna's shaking her head from her perch in the back of the room. Brody's probably paying her to report back, and she's going to tell him I nearly blew this thing before it got off the ground.

The thing about me, the thing nobody believes until

they see it for themselves, is that I cannot tell a lie. If I ever chop down a cherry tree, I'll confess faster than our first president did. People don't believe it. *How can you be an actor if you can't lie?* That's the question they always ask.

The answer's simple. Acting isn't lying. In fact, acting is the most authentic, genuine expression of our humanity. Acting is all about channeling emotions—the actor's real, felt emotions—into a performance.

Lying, however, is outside my skill set. I was raised by a single mom. Lacking the support of family or any nearby friends, she had one hard and fast, set in stone rule: never lie to her. That was it. As long as I didn't lie, she had (and still has) my back. No matter how stupid, dangerous, or ill-advised my behavior was, she supported me so long as I was honest with her.

There were consequences, sure. But she values honesty more than anything else. And it must be hard-wired in my genetic makeup. Because I'm the worst liar you'll ever meet. I ruined the surprise party we tried to throw for Brody, and I told Luna's last lover that her real name is Ann. Every crew member who's ever worked with me has invited me to a poker game.

I'm *that* bad of a liar.

My radical honesty was a known problem for this fake dating plan. I was relying on America's sweetheart to do the heavy lifting. Lia Campbell is decidedly fake. Her commitment to disingenuousness was one of the selling points for me and Brody. We figured she could lie well enough to make up for my inability to sell a falsehood.

But now … I slide Ivy a sidelong glance. Even though she's fast on her feet, she doesn't strike me as a practiced liar.

"Give us a kiss!" the guy from *Entertainment Bytes* shouts, which sets off a chant of *kiss, kiss, kiss.*

Ivy shrinks back.

I pull her close and wrap my arm around her. Thankfully, we'd anticipated this part. While Luna did Ivy's hair and makeup, I'd explained to her that there are ways to pull off a stage kiss without actually making out. Although I'd offered to show her how, she was worried she'd mess it up when the time came.

For this out-of-the blue relationship to be remotely believable, we have to sell the kiss. We both know it.

I turn her to face me and tug her toward me until her hip bones hit my thighs. Then I wrap one arm around her waist and cup her cheek with my free hand.

She stretches on to her toes and then snakes her hands around my neck, tips her chin up, and parts her lips. She's giving me a flashing neon sign that she's good with this.

Still, I double-check. "Sure this is okay?" I whisper, dipping my head.

My mouth so close to hers that her breath is a feather on my lips when she exhales her answer.

"I'm sure."

I move my hand from her hip to her hair and crush my mouth against hers. She leans into me and rakes her fingers through my hair. The flashbulbs are popping off like fireworks. Brody's gonna love it.

Despite the outward appearances of passion, it's a gentle, almost chaste kiss inside our cocoon so I'm surprised when I feel the rapid thrum of her pulse in her throat. Then I feel something much, much worse. And the way her hip bones are pressing into me, I'm afraid she'll feel it through my jeans.

I break contact and pull back, horrified. I have never, not once, gotten aroused on a set. Of course, it has to happen now.

Ivy goes stiff in my arms. I don't blame her. She must think I'm a complete pervert. Time to wrap this up before she freaks out in front of the media.

I clear my throat and play my role. "Thanks for coming out. And while Ivy wants me to invite you all to stick around for tonight's Christmas tree lighting in the town square, I'm going to ask you to respect our privacy. I don't get much time off, and I'm looking forward to using it to make memories with my girl."

I take her hand and lead her to the side door. As arranged, Quinn pulls it open as we approach.

Once we're alone, I turn to her. "I'm sorry."

She bites her lip and drops her gaze from mine. "Forget about it." Her tone is flat.

She turns and crosses the field to the red pickup with the antlers decorating the grille. I want to run after her, make her stop so I can explain, convince her that I'm not an oversexed monster. But the temperature's dropped and neither one of us is wearing a coat. She's shivering, and the wind cuts through my cashmere sweater. I trudge behind her, wishing I could kick my own butt.

By the time I get to the truck, she's in the driver's seat, gripping the steering wheel, and staring straight ahead out the window. I slide onto the bench seat next to her as she turns the key that she left dangling from the ignition.

"The heat'll kick on in a few minutes," she says in that same lifeless voice.

I open my mouth, then snap my jaw closed. Anything I say now is unlikely to make things better and almost certain to make an awkward situation even worse.

She punches the radio button and Christmas music fills the silence between us as she puts the truck into gear and we bump down the gravel hill to the road.

CHAPTER 7

FAUX FUR AND REAL TALK

Ivy

I focus on the road like my life depends on it. My shredded dignity certainly does. One second, I'm kissing Dash, the next he's pulling away from me like I'm poison ivy. I'm so humiliated I don't even laugh at my own corny pun.

My stupidity compounds my embarrassment. Even though my brain knew—*knows*—that the kiss wasn't real, my body and my heart clearly didn't get the memo. As Dash pulled me toward him, cupped my face, and covered my mouth with his, colors whirled behind my eyes, my legs went liquid, and my breath hitched in my chest. I melted into him, forgetting the crowd, the cameras, our arrangement, all of it. I was lost in his warmth, his scent—juniper and cinnamon and something I couldn't place, something uniquely Dash—and the soft pressure of his mouth. I couldn't get close enough, pressing my body against his, winding my fingers through his hair, yearning to consume him.

He could tell. It's not like I hid it. And it obviously disgusts him. The memory of the way he extracted himself from me as if I were toxic stings all over again, and my cheeks blaze. I round my shoulders and curl inward as I pilot the car down the hill and turn onto Lake Road.

I used to do this growing up when my boisterous family got too loud or a good-natured debate between Holly and Merry skated dangerously close to a heated fight. I would pull myself inward, making myself as small as possible in an attempt to retreat from the chaos to the safety of my shell. Mom called me her sneaky snail. Tears sting my eyes at the memory of my mom, and I take a greedy gulp of air.

Dash shifts to face me. "Are you okay?"

"Mmm-hmm." I keep my gaze straight ahead. The only thing that could make this worse would be to break down crying in front of him.

How am I going to get through a whole week like this?

There's really only one way out—and that's through.

I sit up straight, square my shoulders, and stare out the windshield as I say, "I'm sorry. I know the kiss wasn't real. I just … I enjoyed it. That's all."

"Wait." He tugs on the my sleeve. "Look at me."

"Can't. I'm driving." It's true. This road gets icy.

"We need to talk. Can you pull over? Right there." He

points to the right shoulder in front of a red brick house. The entrance to the driveway is flanked by a pair of stone lions.

Involuntarily, I giggle. "Not a good idea. That's Pete and Vicky Swanson's place. Exactly one year ago today, they had my sister's boyfriend arrested for trespassing."

I coast by the rambler and its snow-covered manicured garden while he cranes his head for a better look.

"I thought you said this town is supposed to be friendly."

"It is. Vicky is a special case, but even she's warmed up over the past year. Plus, technically, they don't live in the town proper."

He shakes his head. "We're getting off-topic. Is there someplace we can talk before we go to the inn? Please."

"We can stop at the Snowflake Cafe."

"No. Someplace where we can be alone."

The word *alone* sends a frisson of anticipation through my body even though I have firsthand evidence that he doesn't want to be alone with me for any exciting reason. He probably thinks I'll break down and make a scene when he explains what a fake relationship means.

He's waiting for an answer. I consider banging my head off the steering wheel or veering the truck into the creek to put myself out of my misery. But finally I say, "My dad's fishing cabin isn't far."

"Perfect."

I turn off the road and head toward the woods. We drive in silence across the bridge over Snow Lake and climb the hill to the cabin. I park in the gravel drive next to the wraparound porch.

"This is it." I kill the engine and flip through my dad's keyring until I find the key to the cottage.

Then I climb out of the truck and mount the steps to the porch. Dash follows a few steps behind.

"Aren't you going to lock the truck?" he asks my back while I'm fitting the key into the lock on the front door.

"Look around. There's nobody here, and bears don't generally hot-wire vehicles for joyrides." I glance over my shoulder and give him a small smile. "You're not in Kansas anymore, Toto."

Inside, I stomp my boots on the welcome mat and Dash copies the motion, knocking off the loose snow. Then I flip on the lamp on the side table and eye the fireplace. I doubt we'll be here long enough to merit starting a fire. Instead, I toss him one of the fuzzy fleece blankets that Noelle has scattered around the cabin. My dad's fiancee has a thing for books and blankets. There are piles of both everywhere in the cabin and in their living space at the inn.

I wrap a faux fur pink blanket around me like a cape. He's draped his blanket over his shoulders, too. It's a velvety brown, and it makes him look like a medieval king or warrior wearing the pelt of some beast. All he needs is a turkey drum in his hand and a stein of beer.

I bite back a laugh and gesture toward the couch so we can get this over with.

He shakes his head. "We can't stay long. Brody already leaked the location of the cottage where we're staying to the press. If we don't show up soon, they'll get cold and wander away for a drink."

"Okay. Then say what you need to say. I've already said my piece."

His gaze is intense as he searches my face. "Will you say it again?"

My chest tightens and I rub the blanket's satin edging between my finger and thumb. I say nothing.

"Please. I want to make sure I heard you correctly in the car."

"I enjoyed the kiss, and it was clear you didn't. I know it wasn't real, though. So you don't have to worry." I say the words woodenly.

A smile crosses his lips, but before I can take offense at the implicit mockery, he reaches for the edges of my blanket and pulls me a foot closer to him. Then he lowers his chin and locks eyes with me.

"That's not why I pulled away, Ivy." His voice is thick.

I squint at him. "Really?"

"Really." After a beat he adds, "One thing you need to know about me is I don't lie. Not even when I probably should."

"Then why?"

His chest lifts like he's taking a deep breath. "Because I was turned on, and I was afraid you'd realize and think I'm a perv."

"Wait? What?"

"I got aroused. I didn't expect it. That doesn't happen when I'm acting."

"Never?"

"Never," he confirms.

"Not even on *Vampire Quarterback* when Vlad and Poppy get caught in the rain and—"

"Especially not then. The actress who played Poppy smelled like cured meat."

A laugh explodes from somewhere deep in my belly. It's a big ball of amusement, relief, and wonder. The fact that Dash enjoyed the kiss as much as I did doesn't change anything about our situation, but it makes me feel worlds better.

"Okay. I guess it's a bonus that we don't disgust each other, but …," I trail off, unsure of how to say we have to keep it professional for both our sakes.

"But real feelings are a complication neither of us can afford. We'll save the displays of affection for the public."

I exhale. "Exactly."

He reaches out and tucks a stray piece of hair behind my ear. "This week just got a lot harder, though. Pun intended."

I should step back; I know I should. We just agreed to boundaries. But I don't move.

CHAPTER 8

MEET THE JOLLYS

Dash

Ivy slows the truck to a crawl in front of a stately mansion. The Inn at Mistletoe Mountain's wide front porch is swathed in greens and twinkling lights. A dusting of snow covers the roof. Evergreen wreaths hang from all the windows and two larger wreaths covered in flowers hang from the front doors, which are guarded by a pair of six-foot-tall nutcracker soldiers.

"Wow." It's a clumsy, inadequate response to the emotion the inn stirs up.

She smiles. "I know. Even after all these years, seeing it decorated for the holidays warms me from the inside out."

To my surprise, I know what she means. All I can do is repeat "wow" like a dope.

Then she says, "If it's okay with you, I'll add your large urns from the photoshoot to the porch."

I tear my attention away from the house to blink at her. "What?"

"You're the proud owner of one thousand one hundred and twenty-four fresh flowers, Dash. What do you plan to do with them?"

Leave them in the barn until they die seems like the wrong answer. Underneath my sweater, my shirt collar seems to shrink, cutting off my air supply while my mind races. What *am* I going to do with over a thousand flowers?

I'm about to curse Brody, when Ivy smiles like she's wise to my internal freakout.

"You could donate them to the Mistletoe Mountain Merriment Managers. It's our version of a chamber of commerce. They can dole them out to the various businesses and events to add to their decorations."

"Great idea." I agree to the suggestion instantly, thrilled to have the responsibility for a literal truckload of flowers taken off my hands by a council of elves or whatever they are.

She eases the truck forward and turns into an alley. "We'll park behind the cottage and walk around to the main entrance like regular guests so the press can get some pictures. I'm guessing they're around here somewhere?"

"Probably hiding in the bushes."

She giggles, and I don't have the heart to tell her I'm not joking.

I offer her a hand when she steps out of the pickup truck, then keep her hand in mine as we follow the cobblestone path past the cottage to the walkway around the house to the front. I hear the first shutter click when we draw even with the stand of spruce trees that line the path.

Trees, bushes. I was close enough.

"Is that what I think it is?" she whispers.

I nod, and she nestles closer, her coat sleeve brushing against mine.

Several more photographers, the ones who were smart enough to get out of the cold, scrabble out of two cars parked in front of the inn when they spot us mounting the steps to the porch. At the wide double doors, I turn us around to pose for a clear shot, making sure to position her that so one of her enormous wreaths is visible behind us. Might as well get her some product placement. I flash a smile and give a friendly wave before I push open the doors, setting off a jangle of jingle bells.

I stop just inside the door to stare. The lobby makes the inn's exterior look sedate and sparsely decorated. Everywhere I look I see twinkling lights, fresh garlands and an inordinate number of nutcrackers. The air, warmed by the fire crackling in the fireplace, smells of evergreens, oranges, and cinnamon. Soft music is playing from hidden speakers. It's a cozy, welcoming, scene. I relax my shoulders and loosen my jaw.

My moment of quiet bliss is cut short by a swarm of squealing women. Based on the volume and intensity of the noise, I'd guess there are a dozen of them. But once the swirling bodies settle, there are only three: a blonde and a brunette, both in their twenties, and a woman in her forties. This must be the sisters and their dad's fiancee. The women pepper Ivy with questions, their voices overlapping. I can't make out any of it. Ivy shrinks, rounding her shoulders and ducking her head under the sustained assault of noise.

I wrap my arm around her and snug her into my side. She gives me a sideways glance, probably thinking there's no need to pretend we're dating with them. But that's not why I pulled her close. Instinctively, I want to protect her.

Protect her from her family? Hardly necessary. They're loud—really loud—and excited, but they're not aggressive or overbearing. Still, I felt her discomfort and reacted without thinking. And she nestled into my side like she belongs there.

Before I can continue with my self-analysis, a man strolls out from behind the registration desk to clap my back and shake my hand. His grip is firm but not bone crushing. He smiles, entirely at ease with himself and apparently unfazed by meeting a major movie star.

"Welcome to the Inn at Mistletoe Mountain, Dash."

"Thank you. This place is amazing, Mr. Jolly."

"Wait until you see the cottage. And call me Nick."

He holds out his arms, and Ivy wriggles free of me to hug her father hello.

I turn to find Noelle at my elbow. "Hi. I bet you're Noelle."

"I sure am," she chirps. "Your manager arranged for your bags to be sent over, and someone named Luna dropped off a 'wardrobe' for Ivy." She draws air quotes as she says *wardrobe* and waits a beat before continuing. "Obviously, Ivy knows all the ins and outs around here. But if you need anything, promise you won't hesitate to ask."

"Thanks. And I promise."

I study her for a moment. I know she and Ivy aren't related, but with their red hair, green eyes, and freckles they could be mother and daughter. Ivy's sisters, in contrast, look nothing like her—or each other. One is taller than Ivy and has blonde hair and blue eyes. The other is much shorter with dark curly hair. I'm guessing she's Merry because her jeans are dusted with flour and she's sporting a blue bandage like chefs use around her right ring finger.

I catch Nick's eye. "Can we talk?"

He holds my gaze for an uncomfortably long moment before gesturing toward a door. I feel the women watching us.

"We'll take Ivy to get settled in at the cottage," Holly declares. "Come over when you're done. And bring Jack. He's floating around here somewhere."

As I follow the patriarch through a set of pocket doors, the rest of the Jollys usher Ivy down a long hallway in a cloud of laughter.

Nick leads me to a large kitchen and leans against the center island. "You want some eggnog?"

I've never actually had eggnog. "I'm not sure. What is it?"

He chuckles and opens the refrigerator. "Let's start you out with something easy."

He pulls out two beers, uses an opener stuck to the fridge with a magnet to pop off the caps, and hands me a bottle. He tilts his bottle toward mine and we clink the necks together. Then I raise mine to my lips and take a long pull of cold beer.

"Pretty good." I study the label. "Frosty brown ale. Never heard of it."

"You wouldn't have. Frosty Brewery is local. They host a beer garden after the tree lighting."

I take another swig of liquid courage, then blurt, "Ivy and I aren't really a couple."

He quirks his mouth, then deadpans, "No, really?" He sips his ale. "Did you know Noelle and I signed an NDA? You're supposed to be staying here with Lia Campbell. You can imagine my surprise when you announced that my middle daughter is your girlfriend."

I choke on a mouthful of beer. "I can."

"What happened?"

"I recently starred in a film—"

"*An Inheritance of Irony*. The girls couldn't stop talking about it, so Noelle and I went to see it for date night."

Don't ask.

I ask.

"What did you think?"

"It was a good film. Substantive. It stayed with me afterward. Although your rear end didn't leave the impression on me that it left on my fiancée and daughters."

My spark of pride flickers out, and I wonder if Ivy lied to me.

"All of your daughters?"

He gives me a curious, thoughtful look and is silent for a few seconds. "Come to think of it, that was mainly Holly and Mary. Ivy raved about the movie, but I don't think I heard her talking about your butt."

The flame relights, even brighter.

"They weren't the only ones who focused on my physical attributes rather than my performance, and I didn't handle it as well as I might have."

"That's an understatement."

"So my manager and Lia's hatched a fake romance plan. We were supposed to come here today and announce we've been dating seriously and are taking a break from promoting our movies to spend the week doing … whatever heartwarming Christmassy things people do in Mistletoe Mountain."

"Smart. Cynical, but smart. However, Ivy is not Lia Campbell."

Here we go. I sigh. "Apparently last night I—um—"

"You dropped your drawers in front of the press."

I clear my throat and try not to sound defensive or cowed. "Right, that happened, and as a result Lia backed out of our arrangement. But I was already here, Ivy had already delivered a thousand flowers, and it was too late to cancel on the press. I thought I was cooked. Then I met Ivy.

I realized a real girl next door would make an excellent substitute sweetheart. Am I wrong?"

He gives me a level gaze. "No, you're not. Ivy's the real deal, and being tied to her in this community will make you an instant favorite. I don't know about the rest of the world, and I'm probably biased as her father, but I think she's going to give your image a bump. What's in it for her?"

I stare at him for a long moment, then shake my head. "I don't honestly know, Nick. I did agree to help her with her floral orders because I understand this is a busy time of year. And if she normally pitches in around the inn, I'll be happy to do that, too. But I have no idea why she said yes."

"Carol, Ivy's mom, used to say Ivy collected strays." He laughs.

"Strays?"

"She would bring home injured birds, hungry dogs, and pregnant barn cats. The new, friendless kid at school. A lonely senior citizen whose spouse recently passed away. Her empathy is dialed up to eleven. I suspect she feels sorry for you."

I gape at him. "Sorry for me?" The idea is beyond comprehension. "Nobody feels sorry for a rogue movie star." I should know.

"Ivy would."

"Huh."

Before the idea can sink in, he finishes his beer in one long swallow and rests the empty bottle on the counter near the sink. "Let's get you checked in and rescue Ivy from the gaggle of girls. You can bring your beer."

Instead, I chug the rest of the ale and place my bottle next to his. I follow him outside in a daze. I don't think anyone, ever, has felt sorry for Dasher Pine. I can't wrap my mind around it.

CHAPTER 9

ONLY ONE BED

Ivy

My sisters and Noelle pilot me into the cottage. I stop just inside the door and take it in. Cleaned from top to bottom, the cozy space sparkles. The potted tropical anthurium red splash I gifted Noelle and Dad when they got engaged sits on the side table in a glossy white pot. I'm pleased to see that both the graceful white-striped red blooms and the vibrant green leaves are healthy.

Noelle catches me looking. "We keep it in our bedroom usually. But it's so pretty and rare we decided to move it here to make this place fancy enough for a couple movie stars."

I don't know if what she said lands with my sisters, but

59

it lands with me. I nod and return to checking out the cottage. It's definitely been prepped with Dash (and Lia) in mind rather than the Bryants. Instead of whimsical holiday touches, everything is sleek, elegant, and understated. A glass bowl of vintage silver ornaments occupies the center of the island. A giant three-wick candle from Luminous Lights sits on the mantlepiece. I breathe in the heady mix of cinnamon, pomegranate, and citrus of the shop's best-seller. It echoes the scent of the pomander balls that dangle on satin ribbons from the stocking hangers where Jodi and Mark Bryant usually hang their quilted stockings over the hearth.

I turn to Noelle. "It looks like something out of a design magazine."

Before she can answer, Holly grabs my arm and steers me to the couch. "She's touched. Sit. Spill."

She pulls me down on to the cushion beside her and Merry and Noelle scoot the armchairs closer and lean forward, waiting.

"It's a long story," I begin.

"No, it isn't," Merry says. "In fact, I'll bet it's an extremely short story. You have *not* been secretly dating Dash Pine. I'd know if you were. We live together, remember?"

"Fair," I say. "How was your trip?" I ask Holly.

"It was nice to spend Thanksgiving with Jack's brother and some of their friends."

"What about the evil stepfather?"

"We had lunch with him. He wasn't invited to dinner."

Merry whistles.

I raise an eyebrow. "Harsh."

"He *did* try to steal their mom's empire from them. Now, while I commend the attempt at redirection, let's get back to the pending question." Holly uses her lawyer voice.

"I didn't realize this was a deposition," I stall.

Holly crosses her arms and stares at me.

I bite my lip.

Noelle gives me a close look. "Your father and I had to sign a nondisclosure agreement in order to rent this cottage to Dash. There was a second name on the reservation. And it wasn't yours."

Holly huffs, and I turn toward her again. "Quinn said you reviewed it."

"I did."

"Well, then you know."

Merry puts on her best youngest child pout. "If everybody knows, then you have to tell me. It's not fair. You can't leave me out."

I'm dying to tell her, to tell all of them. But there's one teeny, tiny wrinkle—Merry's big mouth.

I meet Holly's gaze across the room, and she nods like *I've got this.*

"Merry, you can't tell anybody," she warns.

My younger sister has the nerve to look offended when everybody in Mistletoe Mountain knows that the fastest way to spread news is to tell Merry Jolly that it's a secret.

Before she can protest, Holly goes on. "I'm serious. There's an argument that the NDAs extend to whatever it is Ivy's about to tell us. If you share it, Dad and Noelle could be in breach. Ivy, too."

"Okay, okay. I get it."

We all stare at her for a beat.

She raises her hand. "Baker's honor."

"I don't think that's a thing," I tell her.

"It totally is," she lies.

"Just tell us," Holly says, exasperated. "If she blabs, I'll slap a cease and desist on her."

I'm pretty sure this is a bluff. But then, this *is* Holly we're talking about.

"Okay, fine."

In unison, they lean toward me, rapt.

"You know how Dash got a lot of press for his nude scenes in that movie?"

Merry snorts. "Um, yeah."

"That's an understatement," Noelle observes dryly.

"I heard Calvin Klein wants him for a new campaign."

I pause to consider this tidbit of information from Holly before continuing. "He didn't handle it so well."

"You think?" Merry says. "He got hammered on that morning show and went on a rant."

"Not to mention, he mooned some reporters outside a club last night," Noelle adds.

No one would ever accuse the Jolly women of being out of the pop culture loop.

"Right, and until last night, he had a plan to clean up his image by pretending to spend a romantic week in our very own winter wonderland with his longtime girlfriend, Lia Campbell."

"Dash was dating Lia Campbell?" Merry asks, wide-eyed.

"Mmm, no. No, he was not."

Her surprised expression contorts into a scrunched-up, disgusted look. "It was all a PR stunt?"

"Apparently," I say.

"Jack says it's fairly common," Holly informs us.

Jack would probably know. His late mother was an extremely famous author. I note, but don't mention, that Jack could only have weighed in if Holly, Dad, or Noelle spilled the tea despite the NDA. Maybe Merry isn't the only loose-lipped Jolly.

Instead I say, "A public relations stunt that Lia backed out of after Dash's latest behavior."

Merry's catching up. "And you took her spot. How did that happen?"

"Quinn asked me to make these enormous flower arrangements, over a thousand flowers, for a photo shoot. Turns out the photo shoot was going to be Dash and Lia's big announcement about their relationship. I've been awake for almost two days putting together these elaborate flower arrangements."

"We saw the pictures on the internet. They're gorgeous," Noelle says.

If they've seen pictures of the flowers, they've also seen pictures of this kiss. Their *extreme* interest is making even more sense.

"When I was unloading them into Quinn's barn, Dash came outside for some air. I asked him to give me a hand."

"You asked Dash Pine to help you unload flowers from the bed of your dad's pickup truck?" Noelle asks, as if she's misheard me.

"Well, I didn't know it was Dash. He had his collar up and hat pulled low over his forehead. I had my hands full and didn't take a close look at him."

"So then he said, 'I don't do manual labor,' and that's when you found out it was Dash," Holly guesses.

"No, he helped me, and then I recognized him."

"Huh," Holly says.

"It's your meet-cute!" Merry declares.

"It wasn't a meet-cute. It was the beginning of a business arrangement."

"So what happened?" Noelle says. "Did you offer to take Lia's place?"

"No, he asked me. Actually, first he asked me to take my coat off."

"He asked you to take your coat off?" Holly says. "And you did it? That doesn't seem like you."

She's right, of course. "He had just told me Lia backed out and I was panicking. I thought if the photo shoot didn't happen, he might not pay for all those flowers."

"That would be breach of contract, and we would have nailed him to the wall."

"Maybe, but in the moment, I just took off my parka and …"

"He liked what he saw," Merry says.

Blood rushes to my face.

"And cue the blushing."

Noelle throws her a warning look as I barrel ahead with the story. "So he asked. At first I said I couldn't because I have too much work to do."

"You do have too much work to do," Merry says.

Holly and Noelle stare at her.

"It's a crazy time of year. We have a big bulletin board in the kitchen where we have all of our orders pinned up so we don't lose track."

"She's right. Between her desserts business and my flower business, our house is busier than Santa's workshop. But that's not my biggest problem."

"It's not?" Holly asks, calculating lost orders in her head.

"No."

"What is?"

"The sleeping arrangements."

"What?" Noelle says, bewildered.

I look at my soon-to-be stepmother. "There's only one bed."

She laughs. "I'm aware."

Suddenly I remember that she and my dad holed up here for a while the summer she was being stalked.

"What did you do?"

"At that point, your father and I were just friends, so he took the couch."

"*Just friends* is doing a lot of work, but we'll let that go for now," Holly says.

I turn to her. "What did you and Jack do?"

Last year, she shared the cottage with her now-boyfriend before they started dating.

"We had ground rules," Holly tells me.

"Shocker," Merry says.

"We took turns. We alternated getting the bedroom and the couch. But," Holly adds, "that was a different situation."

"How is it different? You weren't dating; we're not really dating."

"*We* weren't dating because I was his court-appointed lawyer and he was my client, and being involved with him would have been a violation of …"

I fade out as she starts naming the rules that she didn't want to violate and snap back to attention when she says, "If I were you, I wouldn't have any ground rules."

"What do you mean? This is a professional situation. We have a boundary."

"What's the boundary?"

"Save the displays of affection for the public. So I guess we should just alternate nights in the bed."

"Or," Merry proposes, "you could throw caution to the wind, acknowledge that you're attracted to each other, and have a fling."

"A fling with Dash Pine?"

"You say it like it's crazy idea."

"It is," I retort.

"No. The crazy idea," Noelle tells me, "would be to not have a fling with Dash Pine."

"Shouldn't you be a good influence on us?"

She laughs. "Your mother raised three amazing daughters. You don't need me to be an influence, good or bad. I'm just saying: it's Dash Pine."

"And we saw that kiss, you know," Holly adds.

"Nothing about it said *professional arrangement,*" Merry agrees.

I'm saved from answering by a knock on the door.

I jump up and practically run across the room.

"That must be Dad and Dash." When I yank open door, there are three men standing on the porch. "And Jack," I add. "Come on in."

They tromp inside and slam the door closed against the cold. While I hug Jack in greeting, Dad shows Dash around the small space.

"Do you want to take off your coats and stay for a drink?"

I haven't opened the refrigerator yet, but I know it'll be fully stocked. That's standard for the inn. Given the guest, they might have upgraded the food and drink, too. Caviar and champagne? Ugh, I hope not—at least on the salty fish eggs.

"We should get back," Dad says. "We still have several guests with late arrivals to check in, and I haven't made the sauce yet."

"My pizza dough should be done rising," Merry tells him.

"Oh, we're not going to be able to come to dinner before the tree lighting."

My announcement lands on my family like a punch.

"It's a tradition, Ivy," my dad says.

"Dad, I know, but we have to go in to the shop. I was gone all day."

"We?"

"Dash is going to help me."

Holly snorts. "Do you know how to do anything in the real world?"

I look at Dash for a second, watching him decide whether to be offended, and I realize it's a fair question.

"The only jobs I've ever had have been acting, serving as a spokesperson, and modeling. I'm not sure they qualify me for much in the real world, but I'm here and I'm willing and able. Ivy can just point me in the direction of what she needs."

Holly nods her approval, and I feel like he's passed the first of what might be several tests from my sisters.

"Do you want me to bring something for you to eat at the festival?" Merry asks.

"No, we'll grab something there."

Noelle wears a small frown but says nothing. Dad wears a bigger frown.

I get out ahead of it. "It won't become a habit. I promise I'll only miss pizza and Negronis before the tree lighting on nights when I'm ambushed into fake dating a movie star."

After a moment, Dad chuckles, Noelle smiles, and the tension evaporates.

CHAPTER 10

EVERY ROSE HAS ITS THORN

Dash

Ivy closes the door behind the Jollys as they leave the cottage and make their way back to the main house in a cloud of laughter and overlapping chatter. She leans her head back against it dramatically, as if she's holding them off physically. After a moment, she shakes out her hands and sighs, then says, "I told you I'm the only quiet Jolly."

"I see what you mean."

"Yeah?"

"Yeah. Like the way you negotiated that interaction. I bet you do that a lot."

She shrugs. "It's part of living in a family. We all have a

role, and mine is peacemaker. Holly's the caretaker, and Merry's the entertainer."

"Does it get old?"

Another shrug.

"They're fun, though."

"Are they?"

Her tone and wry expression make clear she's joking, but I answer her seriously. "Yeah. Growing up as an only child with a single mom, my house was quiet. Too quiet. She worked a lot, and I spent a lot of time by myself."

Her eyes soften, and I frown. I wasn't trying to get her sympathy.

"Oh. I guess I never really thought about how lucky we were. I always craved a quiet place to read a book or just be alone with my thoughts, and with my family and an inn full of guests most of the time, solitude was hard to come by. You always want what you can't have, right?"

I study her mouth. Then her neck. Then the curve of her cheek. I imagine a makeup artist contouring those freckles away, concealing them for the camera. And that would be a shame. She's got the whole girl-next-door thing that casting directors are always looking for and never finding because everyone in LA is trying too hard. Ivy's not trying at all. And she's perfect.

Yeah, I definitely want what I can't have.

She shifts uncomfortably, as if she knows what I'm thinking, and I realize I've been staring at her. I force myself to look away because boundaries, Pine. Boundaries.

I clear my throat. "So now what? Are we going straight to the flower shop or do you need a minute to regroup?"

She raises one eyebrow. "Are you joking? It's like I just told my family. I've been away from the shop all day. We needed to leave ten minutes ago. I have to check my messages, prep tomorrow's arrangements, and then schedule the deliveries. We'll be lucky to get to the town square in time for the tree lighting."

"Sounds like a lot of work."

Then again, my mom used to cram auditions, grocery runs, and her night shift into the same twelve-hour window while I microwaved Hot Pockets alone in our apartment, so what do I know about busy? At least Ivy's got an entire family to lean on. Must be nice.

She shrugs. "I love it."

"Do I need to change?" I gesture at the sweater and dark wash jeans.

"No, but you should find a warmer coat than your leather jacket. Do you have anything? We could borrow something from my dad or Jack."

I wave her off. "I'm sure Luna packed appropriate Vermont mountain wear for me."

"I'm curious what she sent for me. I already have a wardrobe of appropriate Vermont mountain wear."

I laugh. "Trust me, all of it will be completely inappropriate for the weather, but appropriate for magazine covers and viral reels." Male actors are dressed for the weather; female actors are dressed for the male gaze.

Her face pales at the reminder of all the attention that's headed her way, but she presses her lips together and nods.

"Ivy," I say as she wheels the pink hard case toward what I presume is the bedroom.

"Yeah?"

"Thank you."

Her lips soften into a smile.

Ten minutes later, she's changed into jeans and a soft flannel shirt layered over a fitted T-shirt. I'm one hundred percent certain these clothes did not come from the pink case. I think she was wearing them when she delivered the flowers to the barn. Brody and Luna would be appalled, but I like it. She looks real. And touchable.

No touching, Pine.

She pulls on her white parka and a pair of gloves. Her one concession to the wardrobe is to wear the stiletto-heeled boots from our photoshoot rather than the weatherproof snow boots she eyes with longing.

I trade my jacket for the puffy black coat that's currently trending, jam my beanie onto my head, and follow her out the door.

It's a short, brisk walk to Blooms by Ivy, and as we pass the snow-covered storefronts, Ivy points out local businesses—jeweler, coffee shop, social club, soap store. They all sport whimsical names and holiday decorations. Is it quaint? Sure. It could pass for the set of Christmas romance. But how do people actually live here?

"It's charming," I say, and I mean it. "But where do you get groceries or things like paper towels and dog food?"

"There are all the usual big box stores in the valley. It's not a far drive. But the town made a conscious decision to support small businesses, so you'd be surprised at how much you can source right here. Like Three Dog Night Pet Supplies, which carries everything from dog food to kitty litter and saddles. And there's a year-round farmers market on the square where pretty much everyone does their grocery shopping."

"Year round?" I don't hide my disbelief.

"It moves inside the chapel narthax during the coldest months of winter. And during mud season, obviously."

"Mud season? Never heard of it." I tick off the seasons on my fingers. "Winter, spring, summer, fall. No mud season."

"Well, Vermont definitely has mud season. Our fifth season falls between snowmelt in late March or early April and usually wraps up around Memorial Day."

"And it's … muddy."

"To the extreme. All the mud."

I pull a face. "Decidedly less charming."

"We make the best of it. There's even an annual Mud Pie Festival the first week of May."

Assuming that the denizens of Mistletoe Mountain aren't making actual mud pies, I hazard a guess. "Mississippi mud pies?"

She scoffs. "Of course not. Vermont mud pies. Crushed cookies for the crust, covered with a pint each of chocolate and coffee ice cream, topped with chocolate sauce, caramel sauce, and fresh whipped cream. Served with chocolate mousse if you're feeling decadent."

"It sounds both delicious and sickening."

"Right on both counts."

She's still smiling at the thought of the mud pie concoction when we reach the small yellow brick townhouse turned storefront. A blue sign over the door identifies it as Blooms by Ivy. She unlocks the door and waves me inside.

I knock the snow off my boots on the cheerful welcome mat while she turns on the lights and flips the 'closed' sign around to 'open.' I frown at my watch.

"But aren't you closed? It's after five."

"Sure but I was away most of the day for our photo shoot. I can't afford to have someone cover the counter, so if anybody came by while I was closed, they might stop by again before the tree lighting. I'm here. So I might as well stay open."

"That's top-notch customer service."

She shrugs. "Seems like the right thing to do."

She powers up a tablet and opens a spreadsheet, then hands it to me. "This is a list of tomorrow's orders. They're all in the refrigerated case against the wall." She points to a triple-door glass case stuffed full of floral arrangements. "Everything should be set to go, but I was pretty tired yesterday, so we should double check the orders."

"Got it." As I pull open the first door, she turns on a laptop and starts going through emails, typing rapid responses.

When I hear a pause in her typing, I mark my spot on

the order sheet and say, "Mud pies aside, you never wanted to move away?"

Her answer is immediate and unequivocal. "Never. I lived at the inn and commuted to the community college in Stonebridge."

"And your sisters?"

"Holly went to college in Burlington, then law school in New York. She moved back the day after she graduated."

"What about Merry?"

"She didn't go to college. She started baking with our mom when she was three. My dad built her a stepladder so she could reach the counter. She won her first regional competition in second grade. So she convinced our parents to let her use the money set aside for her for college to fund an apprenticeship at a Parisian pâtisserie."

"She knew what she wanted and went for it."

"She did. And she also knew she wanted to bring her fancy French dessert-making skills back home. She runs a dessert truck now, but one day she'll have a real bakery."

We lapse back into silence. I continue to check in orders while she returns several phone calls. When her calls are finished, she joins me at the refrigerated case.

"I'm done with everything else. You read the orders off, and I'll check them. It'll go faster."

I step back. She bends down to retrieve the tablet from the floor, and I admire the view.

She catches me checking her out and shakes her head as she hands me the tablet. "Eyes up here, Dash."

"My bad." I gloss over the awkward moment. "I was just

about to check the Mins' order. It's celosia, salal berries, globe amaranth, and white pine and juniper greens."

She leans into the second case and removes a wreath. "Check."

"This next one is an easy one. Ryan Morgenthal ordered fourteen champagne roses." I look up. "Fourteen?"

"They're for Josh. It's their fourteenth anniversary."

She pulls out a vase and silently counts the pale golden blooms. Then she sticks her face directly into the middle of the flowers and takes a giant sniff.

"Uh, you okay?"

She extends the bouquet. "Smell."

I inhale. Then I stare at her for a few seconds and inhale again, deeper this time. That distinctly rose fragrance is there—and so is something fruity, something sweet, and something spicy.

"What do you smell?"

"Pears." Sniff. "And honey." Another sniff. Then I shake my head. "And some kind of spice. Or maybe licorice?"

"So close. Anise and almond."

"I thought all roses smelled like roses."

"Nope. There are five main categories of fragrances, but roses are complex. More than three hundred compounds layer in different combinations to create dozens, maybe hundreds, of scents." Her voice is tender, almost awe-struck.

I reach out to touch a bloom, and her tone changes. "Careful, they're—"

My finger pricks. "Ow!"

"—a very thorny variety," she finishes as a droplet of bright red blood bubbles up on my skin. Followed by another. And another.

I shake my finger and bite back a curse.

She returns the offending roses to the case and puts a hand on my arm to still it just as I'm about to put my finger in my mouth and suck the blood off.

"Don't," she says as she pulls me into the back room and heads for a utility sink.

"It's a time-honored practice," I tell her. "It's where the phrase 'licking your wounds' comes from."

"Even if that's true, *Vlad*, your mouth isn't sterile."

She turns on the water and tests the temperature before guiding my now freely bleeding finger into the stream. After rinsing it, she washes it with liquid soap, rinses it again, and pats it dry with a soft cloth.

"Do you need a bandage?"

"Nah, I don't think so."

We both lower our heads to take a closer look and our foreheads brush together. She laughs and looks up at me. I smooth that tendril of hair that keeps escaping back behind her ear and watch her throat as she swallows hard.

Her pupils dilate, her breath quickens, and the color creeps up her neck to her face as she arches her back. She's giving me every signal known to man or animal, and my body's responding. Screw boundaries.

I take her face in my hands, dip my head, and part my

lips just as the bells over the store's front door jangle loudly. We jerk apart. My heart races like we almost got caught, but isn't that the whole point?

CHAPTER 11

THE FIRST REAL FAKE DATE

Ivy

By the time I've helped Xander Michaelson pick out the perfect pots of deep red boat orchids and fragrant white hyacinths to complement the seasonal display in the window of his jewelry store, it's almost dark. Dash and I literally dash across town in an effort to make it to the square before Dawn Min throws the switch to light the tree.

We're not quite running, but we're not exactly walking either. It's more of a 1980s fitness-inspired cross between the two with our arms pumping and our feet tapping. Our pace makes conversation almost impossible, which is fine by me because my mind is whirling as fast as my feet in these ridiculous heeled boots. I'm running through our interaction in the back room over and over again.

We came *this close* to kissing. If Xander hadn't walked through the door, we absolutely would have. But we *can't*. We agreed—displays of affection are reserved for the public. And there's nothing remotely public about the windowless back storeroom of my flower shop. Tucked away back there, we might as well have been the only two people in the world. If I didn't fully believe him at the fishing cabin, I do now. He's as drawn to me as I am to him. It's mutual, as wild as that seems.

How can we make it through seven days—and nights— without cracking? I shift my gaze to the side and study his profile. Maybe he can. He's an actor. But I don't know if I can do it.

"Are you good?" He slows his pace to look at me.

Did I say that aloud? After a mortified moment, I relax. He's talking about the race to the square.

"Yeah, it's the boots. We're almost there." I point out the silhouette of the tall tree in the center of town, still visible in the fading light.

He smirks and grabs my hand. "Come on."

We jog the last block together. When we reach the edge of the brick-paved square, we screech to a stop. The crowd is shoulder to shoulder. My family will have a spot right up front, but there's no way we'll be able to swim through all these people before the town manager hits the switch to turn on the lights.

"We'll have to watch from here."

He gives me a disbelieving look and shakes his head. Then he projects his voice to call, "Excuse us," and plunges into the crowd, tugging me along by my hand. The crowd parts to let us through, and dozens of people raise their phones to record our progress. I stare straight ahead and try not to cringe.

Finally, we reach my family, who are not quite front and center—more like slightly to the left, which was always my mom's preferred spot. I squeeze in next to my sisters and Jack and let out a slow breath as my shoulders drop down from my ears. Dash wraps his arm around me and whispers, "It gets easier."

As if she's been waiting for us to get there, the instant we take our spots, the town manager lifts her microphone. "Are you ready to kick off Merriment Month in Mistletoe Mountain?" She pauses for the cheers and shouts before continuing. "This year, Enrique Morales hauled our beautiful twenty-eight-foot-tall tree back from White Pines Tree Farm."

Dawn gestures toward the tree and then toward the far right of the square, where Enrique and his retriever, Bear, stand. Enrique acknowledges the shouts of thanks with a nod. Bear wags his tail.

She continues, "Frosty Brewery has once again graciously sponsored the beer and root beer garden. Look for the heated tent near the chapel. This year the Sober Sleigh rides are courtesy of The Inn at Mistletoe Mountain and Quintessentially Quinn. And, we have special guests to light our tree—Dash Pine and ... um ... our very own Ivy Jolly!"

Dash and I exchange surprised looks. He shrugs, "Brody probably set it up."

"And didn't tell you?"

"I'm sure he sent me a text or something that I ignored. Or Lia's team arranged it."

"Lovely."

"Doesn't matter now—let's go."

He leads me to the platform and shakes hands with Dawn while I blink out at the crowd. When I start to hyperventilate, I remind myself that I know almost every single person looking back at me, and the ones I don't know are vacationers and tourists whom I'll likely never see again. I take a slow breath.

The Mapleville Merrymakers steel drum band plays the opening bars of "Rocking Around The Christmas Tree," and Dash and I reach out together to flip the switch that powers the display. The massive tree lights up with a burst of color, followed by the twinkling white reindeer that prance on the light posts along the square, and finally the lights strung on Santa's gazebo.

He squeezes my hand and cranes his neck to take in the tree. I watch my family's faces light up with joy and pride at the magic that is a Mistletoe Mountain Christmas.

After a moment, he turns his attention to me. "Now what?" he asks, his breath hot on my neck.

"Now we have a beer."

My dad and Noelle beg off to head back to the inn to

tend to their guests. But the rest of us follow the flow of people across the square and into the heated beer tent. The tables are packed in close together and filling up fast. Holly, who ran cross-country and track, sprints across the tent and scores an eight-top. She stands on her toes and waves to her best friend, Delphina, and Delph's boyfriend, Titus, who maneuver through the crowd to join us. They sweep up Quinn along the way.

After shouted introductions, Titus and Jack head to the bar to get a round of drinks while my sisters and our friends join the interminable line for the ladies' room. Dash and I are alone at the table, our heads close together so we can hear each other over the pulse of the DJ's music and the noisy crowd. I lift my chin when I feel someone watching me. Or more accurately, lots of people watching me.

A cluster of my friends and neighbors hover near our table. They elbow one another, whisper behind their hands, and smile at us—at me, actually—like proud parents watching their toddler take her first steps. If it weren't so wholesome and heartwarming, it would be insulting.

Dash notices, too. He takes my hand to his lips and kisses my palm.

"I think they're more interested in you than in me," he smirks. "I didn't know you were a local celebrity."

"Trust me, I'm not. This is small-town life. Everyone knows everyone, and people get heavily invested in anything even remotely interesting. And the two of us as a couple is the hottest gossip since Holly found her ex in the closet with their boss at the DA's Christmas in July office party."

He leans even closer, stares into my eyes, and *smolders*. There's no other way to describe the intensity of his gaze. I'm melting under the heat of it—until I hear the photographers lurking at the edge of the dance floor snapping pictures and remember that this look is for them, not for me.

"Did you just say Christmas in July party?" He asks the question in a normal, non-smoldering voice despite the fact that his eyes are still locked on mine.

I attempt to answer in a similarly casual tone. My voice wavers only a tiny bit when I say, "I did. It's one of my favorite traditions. This month is so busy for everyone living here—with all the visitors who come for the festivities—so we do a second celebration in the summer. What's your favorite holiday tradition?"

He tents his eyebrows and the smolder fades. He opens his mouth to answer but before he gets a word out, Jack and Titus return to the table, both carrying two pint glasses in each hand.

Dash jumps up and relieves them of some of the beers while I place cardboard coasters in front of each seat around the table.

Farah Aboud, home from college for Thanksgiving break, seizes the opportunity to ask Dash for an autograph. He not only signs a coaster for her, he offers to pose for a photo with her. I snap the shot with her phone and she floats away, grinning, as my sisters and Delphina return from the ladies room.

"Did you get lost?" I crack.

"The line was out of control. Merry wanted to use the men's room instead of waiting, but I convinced Marley to open her office up for us," Holly responds to my joke as if it's a legitimate question.

I eye her for a moment. She's been … off … tonight. I thought she was acting spacey at the cottage, too. Maybe it's jet leg. Although Florida to Vermont isn't exactly a long-haul flight.

She pushes her beer away from her, and Jack leans over and whispers something I can't hear in her ear.

"You're sure?" She whispers back.

He nods, and she picks up her glass.

"Are you okay?" I ask her in a low voice.

She lowers her beer from her mouth, leaving a foam mustache. "Of course. Why?"

"You just seem weird."

She pulls a face. "She's probably tired," Jack interjects. "We had a whirlwind trip and a long day today."

Merry and I exchange a look, waiting for Holly to tell her boyfriend she can speak for herself. Instead, she rests her head on his shoulder and says, "That's probably it."

I blink at this uncharacteristic softness but forget all about my older sister when Dash runs his hand up my arm and purr-growls, "Wanna dance?"

I take a long drink of my frosty Frosty's ale and then wipe my mouth. We have a job to do.

I hold out my hand. "I'd love to."

CHAPTER 12

DANCING AROUND THE TRUTH

Dash

I lead Ivy to the crowded parquet dance floor at the front of the tent. The DJ waves energetically to Ivy, light pink box braids bouncing off her tawny brown shoulders, bare in her off-the-shoulder white fur trimmed Mrs. Claus dress, as she dances behind her table.

"Hey, Nebula," Ivy calls to her over the thumping beat.

DJ Nebula winks at her and flashes a sly smile before she leans into her mic and drawls in a voice like honey. "Okay merriment makers, let's slow it down with Leslie Odom, Jr., and Cynthia Erivo's version of 'Winter Song.'"

The bass fades out, and the crowd quiet as the opening strands of the ballad fill the air. Ivy gazes up at me with those impossibly big green eyes. "It's showtime, I guess."

I grin down at her and place my right hand on her hip to tug her toward me. She swallows hard as she rests her left hand on the front of my shoulder. Even in the high-heeled boots, she's not tall enough to reach my neck. The fingers of my left hand and her right weave together as we sway gently to the song's slow rhythm. Her heart beats against my sweater. After a moment, she lowers her gaze and rests her cheek on my chest. Before I can stop myself, I dip my head and breathe in the scent of her warm skin and silky hair.

"You smell like those champagne roses," I murmur against her neck. It's a heady floral scent of spice, fruit, and honey. "Your perfume?"

She laughs, a soft vibration against my chest. "No, occupational hazard."

I inhale again and reflexively press her closer, trapping our hands between our bodies. I forget the cameras, the onlookers, the deal. All I can think about is how much I want her. No, I need her.

The thought is an alarm bell breaking through my desire. *Danger. This woman could destroy you.*

My involuntary groan startles her, and she pulls back, craning her neck to look up at me. "Is something wrong?"

In response I make a throaty sound that could mean anything—or nothing. I swallow and try again. "How long is this song anyway?"

She laughs lightly, and I relax. She hasn't picked up on my panic or my want.

The song finally ends. Before I can lead her off the

dance floor, another song starts up. Another slow one. Ivy moves back into place, her body pressed close against mine and I throw the DJ a look over her head. In return, Nebula shoots finger guns at me and grins like she's doing me a favor. She probably thinks she is.

Three, maybe four, more minutes of torture. I've filmed standing waist-deep in ice water for hours. I can sway with a beautiful woman in my arms for one more song.

I've almost convinced myself when Ivy says, "You never answered me—about your favorite holiday tradition."

I close my eyes for a beat. I'd hoped asking her to dance would get me out of answering this question. Not only did that not work, now I'm once again having to fight my attraction to her. *Great work, Dash.*

Then I mentally shrug. If nothing else, this crappy topic ought to tamp down my desire.

"I don't really have any," I say to the top of her head.

She stops moving in my arms and cranes her neck to study my face. "Not even one?"

"My mom had me when she was nineteen and raised me on her own. Between working nights and spending her days driving me around to auditions and acting classes, she just about had time to make sure I did my schoolwork and all the other parenting things—you know, shopping, cooking, whatever. We didn't have the time, or frankly, the money, to really celebrate the holidays."

"Oh." Her voice is small and sad.

"It was fine. I didn't know any different when I was

younger. And then once I landed the role as Vlad, we traveled on winter breaks."

She's quiet for a moment, considering this. "What about your grandparents?"

"What about them?"

"You didn't spend holidays with them when you were little?"

"She moved to Los Angeles when she was eighteen, the day after she graduated high school. Her parents weren't thrilled about that. Then when she got pregnant and decided to keep me, they disowned her."

She squeezes my hand and makes a little sound.

My voice flattens as I force out, "I've never met them."

"Dash, I'm so sorry." She traces a slow circle on my chest with her palm, like she's soothing a baby.

"Don't be," I grit out. "I can't miss them. I never knew them."

"Mmm." She catches her lip between her teeth as she weighs her next question. "Your dad didn't—wasn't involved?"

"I don't know who my father is."

She shakes her head. "I don't understand. Your mother never told you his name?"

"No."

"What does it say on your birth certificate?"

"Father unknown."

"Is he?"

"Unknown? Not to her. But she's adamant that there's

no need to know anything about him. He chose not to have anything to do with us."

Her voice wobbles. "Dash—"

We're no longer dancing, just standing stock still in the middle of a crowded dance floor in a crowded tent with hundreds of pairs of curious eyes trained on us. I lower my voice, "I'd really rather not talk about this. Not here, not now."

She frowns and stiffens in my arms. "Okay, I'm sorry. But …."

I wait, but she doesn't continue. "But what?" I finally prompt her.

"You said that you never lie to your mother."

"That's right."

She stretches up onto her toes and presses her cool hands against my burning face. "But you're not completely honest with her either. You haven't told her that her decision isn't fair to you. You haven't told her that you're hurt, that you deserve to know who your father is, at a minimum."

My jaw tightens as the words hit like a gut punch. It's the raw truth, plain and clear. And it hurts like hell.

Maybe that's why I lower my mouth to her, fierce with need. Or maybe it was inevitable all along. Either way, I push the words from my mind as I probe her welcoming mouth with my tongue, tasting the sweetness of her. This isn't for the cameras, this is for me.

❄

When I regain control of myself, the first thing I notice is the stillness. There's no music. DJ Nebula is gawking at us, along with the rest of town and the press. I catch her eye and she hurriedly queues up a banger. The world starts turning again. Conversations resume.

Ivy and I are still entwined. I ease her hands from my shoulders and she steps back quickly. Her chest heaves. I've managed to destroy her updo. Strawberry blonde waves fall over her face like a curtain. Her lips are swollen. Her head is down, so I can't see her face, but the smart money says she's flushed.

Before I can say a word, she pushes her hair out of her eyes and looks up. "Do you think they got what they needed?"

I have no idea what she's talking about. I give her a blank look. "Who?"

"The photographers?" She frowns, confused by my confusion.

Ice water flows through my veins, dousing the heat we created. Right. The press.

"Oh, yeah. Definitely."

She turns her mouth up into a small smile.

Merry shimmies across the tent in time to the music and plants herself in front of us. "We're bouncing to Rudy's. You guys in?"

I glance at Ivy.

"It's a dive bar," she explains. Then she turns to her sister. "Who's we?"

"Quinn, Delph, Titus, and me."

"Holly and Jack aren't going?"

Merry rolls her eyes. "They begged off. Jack says she's tired."

Ivy purses her lips, and some silent sibling communication passes between them. After a moment, Merry says, "Exactly."

"If you want to go along, have at it," I tell Ivy. "I'm going to take pity on the press and go back to the cottage."

"Come again?" her sister asks.

"They can't call it a night until I do."

Merry wrinkles her nose. "Eww, so they're hanging around hoping you show your butt again?"

"Pretty much—literally and metaphorical." I shrug. "It's their job."

Every celebrity who bitterly dismisses the media as parasites is either a hypocrite or confused about the nature of the symbiotic relationship in question. It's not parasitic, it's obligate mutualistic. We need each other. Without us, there's no story. Without them, there's no attention.

Ivy gives me a look I can't read and says, "I'm going to turn in, too. It'll look bad if I go out partying without my *boyfriend* on his first night in town."

She has a point. Even Merry nods in agreement, although she makes sure to call us lame before she hugs Ivy and flits off.

Back at our table, I ask, "Is there anybody you want to say goodbye to?"

She shakes her head. "No."

I hold her coat for her and she wriggles into it. A pair of photographers start snapping pictures. I can see the headline now, "Dashing Dash Shows Chivalry Survives." If there's one thing entertainment reporters love, it's alliteration.

I grab her hand and lead her to the cluster of photographers. "Hey, we're calling it a night. You can feel free to follow us back to the cottage and stand around freezing your butts off. Or you can clock out and have a free beer. I recommend the Frosty lager."

The bearded guy, whose name is Raj or Ron, something short that starts with an R, grabs his camera bag from the floor. "Sounds good to me."

A stringer for a gossip website wants one last shot. " Come on, Dash, Ivy, give us one more kiss," he wheedles.

I'm not about to subject her—or myself—to another kiss when I've barely recovered from the last one.

"We're tired, folks." I turn to leave but Ivy tugs on my arm.

When I look back at her, she points to the tent's roof. "We're under the mistletoe."

Sure enough, a full sprig of the stuff hangs from the canopy by a red velvet ribbon. It's directly over our heads. I search her face and she gives me the tiniest nod.

Okay then, we're doing this.

"What are the odds?" I crack.

"The odds are excellent," she informs me. "It hangs all over town all month long."

Raj/Ron grabs his bag and takes out the camera he just put away. Once they're ready to capture the shot, I turn her in my arms so that the twinkling lights play over her face. She tips her head back and I swoop in for the kiss.

Her lips are unyielding this time. I get it. I cup her cheeks and she stretches up to wind her fingers through my hair. I smile against her mouth. She's a natural. She instinctively understands the kiss can be chaste so long as the rest of our body language tells a different story.

I concentrate on the flashbulbs, the music, the crowd. Anything but the woman in my arms.

After a beat, we break apart.

"Good night," she says with a warm, open smile. The press eats it up. She's fresh-faced and real, completely different from the polished pros they're used to.

When we leave the tent, the wind's picked up. Blowing snow stings my face, and I lower my head against it.

"It's a short walk," she promises. Then, "There's only one bed."

I'd noticed. Believe me, I'd noticed.

"I'll sleep on the couch," I tell her.

"We'll take turns."

I frown at this. "We'll figure it out once we're inside."

We cover the rest of the distance in silence. When we reach the path to the cottage, she breaks into a jog and I follow suit. She punches in the code to unlock the door and we hurry in from the cold.

She kicks off her boots and stows them on a shelf built into the base of the bench beside the door. I do the same with my shoes and take off the ski jacket. She strips off her parka and hangs it on the coat rack. Her teeth chatter.

"Do you want me to make a fire?" I ask, rubbing my hands together and pointing my chin toward the fireplace.

She raises an eyebrow. "You know how to make a fire?"

"Cody Jones makes a fire after he leaves the ranch to wander," I remind her.

"You made *that* fire yourself?"

"Well, no," I allow. "But I learned how to make one. The closeup of Cody's shaking hands, that's me. But the director wanted a really big, impressive fire so the pyrotechnics team enhanced it."

She smiles and leans against the kitchen island. "I want to see this. You make a fire, I'll make us some tea."

"Deal."

I crouch in front of the hearth and reach for the kindling while she fills the kettle with water, softly humming to herself.

A white flash outside the big window over the couch pulls my attention away from the fire. In the kitchen, Ivy shrieks my name and points toward the window and the dark night beyond. I wheel around in time to see Shane Nottingham's pale face in the glass. Nottingham is a true weasel. The kind of paparazzo who would snap pictures of models sunbathing topless in their own backyard, chase a car through a tunnel, or have no qualms about following a celeb's kid to school. He *is* a parasite.

A fireball of rage roars through my belly. I grip the fireplace poker in my hand and explode to my feet. I yank open the door and tear outside in my socks, snarling Shane's name. He jumps down from the ledge, crashes through the hedgerow, and flees behind the Jollys' garage. I chase him down the snowy alley until he vanishes from sight.

I stand, panting and seething, for a long moment. My heart thuds as adrenaline washes over me in waves.

By the time I come back inside, I've cooled down.

"I'm sorry," I say to Ivy in a calm voice as I peel off my sopping socks. "He's known for stunts like that."

She hands me a mug, and I wrap my cold hands around the hot ceramic. "It's not your fault. But I guess taking turns on the couch isn't going to work. At least not until we get a window covering."

CHAPTER 13

ALSTROEMERIA, BEGONIA, CHRYSANTHEMUM. LAWN CLIPPINGS.

Ivy

I lie on my back and stare up at the ceiling in the dark. On the other side of the pillow barrier we've built, Dash breathes evenly. He fell asleep the moment his head hit the pillow. Meanwhile, I'm wide awake on my side of Mount Pillow, stiff as a board. I'm so rigid that it reminds of the sleepover game Holly, Merry, and I used to play with our Field cousins when they visited. The six of us would play "light as a feather, stiff as a board" in our pajamas, giggling and waiting to see who would levitate. I smile at the memory.

I have to get some sleep. But I'm hyperaware of the man I'm sharing a bed with. Also, I'm hot. Boiling, even. My strategy for getting through the night with some semblance of propriety was to pretend I was a Victorian era woman protecting modesty with layer upon layer of clothing. That said, the cottage heats efficiently thanks to the remodel my dad and mom did several years ago, and radiant heat pours into the room, making my sweatpants, long-sleeve shirt, and sweatshirt a poor choice.

This is ludicrous. I'm sweating buckets, and he's sound asleep. I ease myself out from under the covers and wriggle out of the sweatshirt one arm at a time and then lower my sweatpants over my hips. I also shed the fuzzy socks, tossing my fleece suit of armor onto the floor.

In a tee shirt and panties, it's about a million degrees cooler. But I'm still too keyed-up to sleep. I roll over with my back to Dash and use my dad's trick. He once told me that when he needs to try to fall asleep or distract himself, he lists off hotels in alphabetical order and rarely gets as far as the Mandarin Oriental before he falls asleep or forgets what's bothering him.

I don't know that many hotels, but I can list flowers with the best of them. Alstroemeria, begonia, chrysanthemum. Daffodil. English rose, freesia, gardenia. Hyacinth, iris, jasmine. I'm trying to think of a flower that starts with K, when my heavy eyelids close, my brain shuts off, and I drift to sleep.

Six hours later, my eyes pop open and I exclaim, "Kalmia!"

In response to my excited shout something warm moves against my bare stomach. I look down. Dash's arm is wrapped around my waist, my shirt scrunched up. My back presses into his front and his nose nestles on my neck. We're spooning.

What the frost? I scrabble upright. He rolls away with a sleepy sigh.

My gaze falls to the floor. Our pillow border is strewn around the bed. Bolsters and shams litter the floor.

Oh.

Beside me, Dash reaches his arms overhead and stretches languidly like a cat then rolls back to face me with a half-awake smile. "What's kalmia?"

"It's a flower—commonly called mountain laurel. It's usually white, pink, or red," I mumble, mortified. I reach over the edge of the bed and pluck my sweatpants from the floor, then rustle into them under the covers.

He watches me for a moment, bemused, and then laughs. "Looks like our pillow defense system failed."

He throws back the covers, and my mortification ratchets up to an eleven out of ten. Apparently I'm not the only one who got hot during the night. He's shirtless. And when he stretches again, his core engages and his defined abs tighten. I squeeze my eyes shut as if there's any chance I'll be able to unsee his perfect six pack. Then I turn to the wall, open my eyes, and race into the bathroom.

By the time I've washed my face, brushed and flossed, and dragged a comb through my unruly hair, my rolling boil of embarrassment has dropped to a low simmer. I square my shoulders and reluctantly force myself to leave the bathroom.

I follow the smell of coffee into the kitchen, grateful

and curious. Holly says you can tell a lot about a person by how they take their coffee. I wonder if Dash takes his black or with lots of cream and sugar.

When I step into the kitchen, he's leaning against the counter, still shirtless, his sweatpants low on his hips. But I fixate on his drink. He's sipping something bright green from a glass.

"Thanks for starting the coffee."

He tips his glass at me in response and hands me a mug of coffee, steam rising from the surface.

"What is *that*?" I jerk my chin toward his beverage.

"An iced matcha wheatgrass latte."

If that's a latte, I'm Cindy Lou Who. "Are you being punished?"

He laughs. "You get used to the taste. Want a sip?"

"Pass."

"How do you know you're not missing out on something delicious?"

I side-eye the green stuff again. "I'm willing to take that risk. Where did you even get that?"

"I brought it with me. I wasn't sure if I could find everything I needed here."

I stir a spoonful of sugar into my coffee, raise the candy-cane striped mug to my lips, and savor my first swallow of hot, caffeinated goodness while I think. "Mountain Organics might have what you need. It's a small grocery co-op on High Street. They have limited shelf space, but they'll special order if you ask them to."

"Cheers to Mountain Organics." He tips his glass toward me.

I clink my mug against it, then blurt, "Are we going to talk about what happened last night?"

"What happened last night?"

Is he serious? "Didn't you notice? We woke up spooning."

"We were asleep." He chugs the electric green concoction. "It's not like we did it on purpose."

I consider this. He's right, of course. But it still feels vaguely wrong. "Still …"

"Still, what?"

I fight the urge to tell him never mind. Instead I say, "I need clearly delineated lines. I understand that what we do in public isn't real. But"—I take a breath—"I'm not built for a no-strings fling. We have to maintain boundaries."

His eyebrows shoot up and he rakes his fingers through his sleep-mussed hair. He's silent for what feels like hours. I drink my coffee and try not to jump out of my skin.

Finally he says, "Of course. We'll get a curtain for the living room today."

His tone is curt, and I'm confused. Is he upset?

But in the next instant, he grins. "What's on the agenda for today?"

I must have imagined it. "Today we're going to White Pines."

"What's White Pines?"

"It's a Christmas tree farm in the valley. Every year, the

day after the Christmas tree lighting, we go to White Pines Farm and cut down two trees."

"Why two?"

"We get a giant one for the foyer of the inn. We invite guests to help decorate it all month long. And then we pick out a more reasonably sized tree for the family living quarters. We'll decorate that one tonight, just us."

He frowns. "I'll come along to the tree farm, but I don't think I should join you to decorate. It sounds like a family activity."

"Jack will be there," I counter.

"As far as I know he's your sister's actual boyfriend. You just said we need to have boundaries." He blows out a frustrated breath.

"I did say that," I concede. Then I place the mug on the island and put a hand on his bare arm. "I don't know what we are exactly, but I'd like to be friends. It's the holidays, and I won't let a friend miss out on the celebration."

He opens his mouth and I raise my free hand like a crossing guard. "Before you say you can't miss what you never had, that's not true. You've been missing something special. Not this year. Decorating the tree is fun. Noelle's going to make Negronis since we missed them last night. We'll eat too many cookies, tell stories, and trim the tree."

He softens his shoulders as if he might cave, so I move in for the kill.

"Tell you what. If you try tree decorating, I'll try an iced matcha wheatgrass latte the next time you make one. Then we'll both find out what we've been missing. Deal?"

He eyes me. "Really?"

"Really," I lie. I'll find a way to back out later. What's he going to do, undecorate the tree tomorrow when I don't drink it?

"Then we have a deal."

I beam at him. "Perfect."

He smiles back, then pads across the room and reaches into the refrigerator. When he turns around, he's holding a blender full of the green stuff.

He grabs a glass, fills it with ice, and pours the abomination into it.

"Thanks," I say weakly as he hands it to me.

I sniff it cautiously. It smells like grass.

"Bottom's up."

I scowl at him and put the glass to my lips. Then, I silently chant the rhyme my mom used to say to get my sisters and me to swallow medicine when we were little—*Over the lips, past the gums; look out stomach, here it comes!*—and take the world's smallest sip. In the least surprising development of the day, it also tastes like lawn clippings.

Dash is smirking at me. "What's the verdict?"

I put on a snooty tone, swirling the liquid in my glass while I say, "Very grass-forward with undertones of dirt and hay and a vegetal finish."

When he doubles over laughing, I quickly dump the rest of the drink into the sink.

CHAPTER 14

FRIEND ZONED

Dash

White Pines Tree Farm is straight out of a Hallmark movie. There's a rustic barn, a red tractor pulling a wagon filled with pink-cheeked families perched on hay bales, and the sound of squealing children and barking dogs. The scent of fresh-cut pine and woodsmoke mingles with spiced cider wafting from the refreshment table beside the barn. I've been on movie sets that I thought captured this kind of magic. Now, though, I realize it was only a weak imitation.

Beside me, Ivy inhales deeply, and her face lights up with quiet joy. I want to make her smile this way every day. The thought startles me. Then I remember with a pang—

friends. It doesn't matter what I want. She wants something else. Friendship. Boundaries.

"Are you coming, Dash?" Noelle calls.

I've stopped walking. I shove aside the sting of reality and follow the Jollys through the rows upon rows of trees that stretch up the hillside. We stop by a row of tall, elegant firs.

Ivy looks over at me. "We always get one of these for the inn. Concolors hold their needles for a long time and"—she breaks a needle off the closest tree and crushes it between her gloved fingers—"they smell like oranges."

I cock my head, not sure if she's serious.

"Here, smell." She crunches through the snow and holds the needle out for me to take.

Instead, I wrap my fingers around her wrist and bring her hand up to my face. I inhale, and the aroma of citrus fills my nose. Her pulse rate is fast under my fingers, and my own heart races in return. I hold her near me for a beat too long before gently removing my hand.

She swallows hard and looks away, but not before I see the color creeping up her neck. The Jollys settle on a twelve-foot tree for the foyer and tag it to be cut down by the workers.

"Now, it's time to pick the important one," Holly tells me.

Noelle and Nick lead the family further up the hill, fingers entwined. Nick carries a saw. Merry bounces between trees, her laugh echoing across the hillside as she touches one snow-dusted branch after another, declaring each "the one" before moving to the next. Holly follows with a measuring tape, calling out dimensions. Jack trails behind her with a tender smile that says he'd follow her anywhere.

Then there's Ivy. She crinkles her eyes when she laughs at her sisters. Reflexively brushes pine needles from Noelle's shoulder. Points out a cardinal to Jack. She's the quiet center of this solar system, the gravity that holds them all together.

I want to be in her orbit. This morning she woke up in my arms, warm, soft, and relaxed, and I felt peace. At least for the ten seconds before she realized where she was and scrambled out of reach. And reset our boundary. *Friends.*

I never have women spend the night. The optics are too risky, and, if I'm honest, it's always seemed too intimate—way more than sex. But I loved waking up next to a sweat-suit-wearing weirdo who mumbles names of flowers in her sleep.

"Dash, come settle this!" Nick waves me over to the group.

Holly's measuring a towering Douglas fir. Merry's pushing for a fat Fraser fir that's wider than it is tall. They're not actually arguing. I'm learning this is how the Jollys communicate, through affectionate bickering that somehow ends in consensus.

"You're the tiebreaker," Nick declares. "Which tree?"

Six sets of eyes land on me. You'd think it would feel

uncomfortable, being put on the spot. Instead, it feels like … family.

Ivy hasn't weighed in, but she runs her hand over the branches of a medium-sized blue spruce. No bare spots, a perfectly straight trunk, and glossy needles. It's understated and beautiful—like her.

I point to it. "That one. The one Ivy likes."

She snaps her head toward me. Surprise and delight that I really see her flicker across her face before she smooths her expression to neutral and looks away.

Right. Friends.

Nick claps my back. "Good eye, son."

Son. The word lands like a punch.

Before I can unpack the three letters, he passes me the saw. "You do the honors."

I crouch in the snow beside the blue spruce and prop the saw against the trunk. Its teeth bite into bark. Pine sap sticks to my gloves. Each pull of the blade releases more of that sharp, clean scent.

The Jollys cheer me on.

"You've got it!"

"Almost there!"

For a moment I'm not a grown man sawing through eight inches of wood with a flimsy saw. Instead it's my first bike ride, my first day of middle school, my first baseball game. Every childhood milestone I never had collapsed into this moment.

The tree shudders. Ivy lunges forward to steady it as it drops into my arms.

The spell breaks, but I'm still grinning like an idiot, breathless and ridiculously proud of myself for cutting down a tree. Ivy's grinning back, sticky needles in her hair, her eyes bright and her cheeks pink from the cold. And for one moment, I let myself pretend that I can have this life. Then I look away.

On the walk back to the barn, the sisters insist on carrying the tree, per tradition. Jack and I trail behind and listen to their laughter, singing, and a squabble about whether Taylor Swift really grew up on a Christmas tree farm in Pennsylvania.

"She did, you know," I tell Jack.

"It doesn't matter. They had the same debate last year, and I pulled out my phone to settle it with an internet search but they stopped me."

"Why?"

He chuckles. "They don't want to know the answer because then they won't be able to fight about it anymore. They aren't even consistent. Holly said they argue different sides some years."

I'm mystified in silence. After a moment, I say, "I guess I don't get it because I'm an only child."

Jack gives me a friendly shoulder bump. "I have a brother, and I don't get it. The Jollys are different. Or at least they're different from my family. My parents split up when my brother and I were really little, then our dad died. So for a long time, it was just us and our mom. She raised us alone, worked full-time, and had a side hustle."

I eye him. "That sounds an awful lot like my childhood."

"Without the teen heartthrob status, you mean." He says it lightly, jokily.

But I answer seriously. "That was my job. My childhood was … nothing like this, that's for sure."

"Want some advice?"

"Sure."

"Let it wash over you. Don't worry about doing the right thing or doing *anything*. Just be. That's what they do."

"Just be."

"Exactly." He nods sagely.

When we reach the clearing, Nick takes the tree from his daughters and heads into the barn to pay for it and get it tied up for the trip home. The rest of us gather around the crackling bonfire. Noelle passes around cups of hot cider, and Merry recounts the story of the year they dropped the tree on Holly's foot, fracturing it, and she insisted on running the annual holiday 5K in a walking boot.

Jack nuzzles her neck and calls her a warrior princess.

"I am," Holly agrees. "But I regretted my choices when my toenails turned black. I couldn't wear sandals that whole next summer."

"It was so disgusting," Merry cackles.

Ivy laughs at the memory and leans into me, her head on my shoulder, and the weight of it feels right. Like she belongs there.

Then she snaps out of it and straightens, putting careful distance between us on the log where we sit. Is it weird that I feel her absence even though she's a foot to my right?

I look down at the steam coming off my mug.

Right. Friends.

When I sip the cider, it tastes like apples and cinnamon and everything I never had.

CHAPTER 15

TWO (SECRET) WEDDINGS AND A ROMAN SHADE

Ivy

The family room glows with firelight and the soft twinkle of the white lights strung on the seven-foot blue spruce that Dash cut down this afternoon. The tree *I* wanted stands in front of the mullioned windows, and boxes of ornaments cover every surface—the coffee table, the side tables, even the ottomans. Fuzzy blankets drape over the backs of chairs and the arms of sofas. Wicker baskets full of books and board games compete for space with fragrant candles and more than a dozen whimsical nutcrackers. It's cozy. It's inviting. It feels like home. I wonder what it feels like to Jack and Dash.

Noelle passes around pink Negronis in rocks glasses garnished with orange slices. Holly opts for a glass of sparkling mineral water instead and settles onto the loveseat beside Jack.

Dash stands near the tree, holding a delicate glass ball painted to look like a cardinal. "Where does this one go?"

"Anywhere you want," I tell him. "There's no wrong place."

He studies the tree with the intensity of someone defusing a bomb, then carefully hangs the ornament on a branch at eye level.

Merry snorts. "You put all the pretty ones at eye level. Ivy's going to move them around after you go to bed."

"I will not," I protest.

"You absolutely will," Holly agrees. "She has a system," she adds approvingly to Jack and Dash.

"There's no system," I insist, even though there definitely is. Ornaments should be distributed by color, size, and sentimental value to create visual balance. This is basic decorating.

Dash grins at me. "Should I be taking notes?"

"Ignore them. You're doing great."

And he is. Watching him handle each ornament with care, asking about the stories behind them, laughing at Merry's chaotic hanging style—he fits here. Like he's always been part of our weird, loud family.

Dad hands him a wooden ornament carved to look like a stack of books. "Carol made this one the year Noelle came to back to town for good to run the library. She loved that her best friend was back."

Dash turns it over in his hands, studying the detail. "She was talented."

"She was," Dad agrees quietly.

The moment stretches, comfortable and sad at once, until Merry breaks it by hanging three ornaments on the same branch.

"Structural integrity, Mer," Holly calls.

"I'm creating a vignette."

"You're creating a problem," I tell her.

I catch Dash's eye and he mouths, "Vignette?"

I shrug. With Merry, who knows?

An hour later, the tree is decorated. We settle in. Dad and Noelle in their usual spot on the sofa, Merry curled up in the wingback chair, Holly and Jack snuggling on the loveseat. Dash and I share an oversized ottoman, several careful inches of space between us.

Dad raises his glass. "Before we call it a night, how about three things? Since we didn't eat dinner together."

"Yes!" Merry bounces in her seat.

The ritual is so familiar, so comforting, so integral to who I am, who we all are. This feeling of belonging is what I wanted for Dash when I insisted he join us tonight.

Dad goes first. "I'm grateful we're all together tonight. I regret not finishing the manger I started making before your Mom got sick—I keep meaning to complete it and never do. Tomorrow, I'm going to spend an hour in the workshop and make progress on it."

Noelle reaches over and squeezes his hand. "I'm grateful we can continue old traditions and start new ones.

I regret being short with Mrs. Henderson when she complained about the water pressure—she's lonely, and complaining is how she connects. Tomorrow, I'll invite her to join me for afternoon tea."

Merry sips her Negroni. "I'm grateful for this chaos, even when Holly and Ivy are being bossy about my vignettes. I regret eating an entire batch of cookie dough for lunch instead of actual food. Tomorrow, I'm going to meal prep so I stop doing that."

"You say that every week," Holly observes.

"And every week I mean it."

Holly smiles and launches into hers. "I'm grateful for Jack and for you goofballs. Did you know last night was the one-year anniversary of the day Jack and I met? Which leads me to my regret. I regret keeping a secret from everyone." She pauses, and something passes between her and Jack. "And tomorrow, I'm going to ... well, actually, we have something to tell you tonight."

The room goes still.

Jack takes Holly's hand. "We got married. Last week, in Florida."

For a beat, nobody moves. Then Merry shrieks—actually shrieks—and launches herself at Holly, nearly knocking over Jack's drink. Dad and Noelle are on their feet, pulling them both into hugs. I'm slower to react, my brain trying to catch up.

Married?

Holly's laughing and crying at the same time as Merry

demands to see the ring. Jack explains that he gave Holly his mother's ring and it's at Alpine Jewelers being resized.

Noelle asks about the ceremony. Holly says they did it at the courthouse with Jack's brother as a witness.

"But why?" I finally manage.

Jack explains. His brother's moving to England to manage their mother's European publishing interests. Jack's taking over the Florida operations, and he and Holly will have a long-distance relationship for at least a year, maybe longer. "We wanted to be official, legally tied to each other, before the chaos begins," he says, rubbing his hand over Holly's palm.

"We're planning to do a real wedding here later," Holly adds quickly. "For the town, for you guys. This was just for us."

"Like eloping," Merry says dreamily. "How romantic."

"So romantic I'm going to need you to throw me a party anyway," Holly tells her. "I want the whole town to celebrate with us."

"Done," Merry agrees. "I'm thinking a Valentine's Day theme—"

"During mud season? Absolutely not."

Dad clears his throat. "Well, since we're sharing secrets …"

Noelle's cheeks turn pink. "Nick—"

"They should know, Noe." He looks around the room. "Noelle and I got married, too. Right after Christmas in July. Judge MacIntosh performed a private ceremony at the cabin."

This time, I'm the one who shrieks.

The room erupts again—more hugs, more questions, more laughter. Why didn't they tell us? Why so secretive?

"Because we didn't want the fuss," Noelle explains. "It was just for us. Nothing official-official. No rings, no name change. Just us, married."

"Nothing official-official?" Holly sputters. "Marriage is literally the definition of official!"

"You know what I mean."

"We're throwing you a reception," Merry declares. "Both of you. All four of you. A massive party."

Noelle holds up her hands. "After Holly and Jack's party. I don't want to steal their thunder."

Merry flops back in her chair dramatically. "Fine. I guess I need to 'fess up. I'm also secretly married." She cackles at our expressions. "Just kidding! But honestly, at this rate, I might be the only single Jolly left."

"Um, hello?" I say. "Remember me?"

Every member of my family, including my brand-new brother-in-law look pointedly at me, then Dash, then back at me. And I, of course, blush furiously. Dash is all smiles.

The celebration continues—more toasts, more stories about the secret ceremonies, more plans for parties. I smile and laugh in all the right places, but something's shifting inside me.

Holly took a risk. She married Jack knowing they'd be apart, that it would be hard, that there are no guarantees.

Dad and Noelle did what felt right to them, traditions and expectations be damned.

Merry, well, she's infamous for jumping into the unknown and trusting she'll land on her feet.

Everyone's being brave. Everyone's taking leaps. Everyone's choosing love over fear. Everyone but me.

I've spent my whole life being the quiet one, the careful one, the one who doesn't make waves. The peacemaker. The safe choice. And where has it gotten me?

I glance at Dash. He's listening to Jack describe the courthouse ceremony, asking questions, genuinely interested. He fits here. He's relaxed and happy and more himself than I've seen him.

What if I took a risk? What if I told him I don't want boundaries after all?

It's only a week. But what if—?

"Ivy?"

I snap back to attention. Dad's looking at me expectantly.

"Sorry, what?"

"Your three things?"

Oh. Right. I've been so busy processing everyone else's reveals that I forgot we hadn't finished the ritual.

"Um. I'm grateful that Dash is here experiencing this." I feel him turn toward me but keep my eyes on my dad. "I regret being too cautious sometimes. And tomorrow"—I take a breath—"I'm going to take a risk."

"That's the spirit," Merry cheers.

Dad nods approvingly, and Noelle gives me a shrewd look. She knows. Somehow, she always knows.

"Dash?" Dad prompts. "You're up."

Dash shifts beside me. "I'm grateful you included me tonight. Thank you." His voice roughens, just a bit. "I regret making Ivy taste my matcha wheatgrass latte in exchange for my presence."

"You didn't?" Merry gasps.

I elbow him gently. "It wasn't that bad. No, yeah, it was."

When the laughter dies down, he continues. "And tomorrow, I'm going to make myself useful. Pop into some of the shops in town, meet more people, maybe charm some of the inn's guests. Might as well use my celebrity status to help out while I'm here."

Dad beams. "That's generous of you, son."

There's that word again. Dash's face tightens with emotion before he hides it behind his Negroni.

An hour later, Dash and I are walking back to the cottage. The temperature has dropped, and our breath makes clouds in the air. I pull up my parka hood to cover my cold ears.

"Your family is so welcoming," Dash says.

"They're a lot."

"They're perfect." He's quiet for a moment. "Watching your dad and Noelle, seeing how happy they are, and knowing that Holly and Jack took such a huge leap even though long-distance is terrifying shows how much support you all give each other. It lets them take risks, you know?"

I do know. It's exactly what I was thinking.

"What would it be like to have that? That solid foundation and the certainty that someone has your back no matter what?" He laughs, but it sounds hollow. "Sorry. That got heavy."

"No, I get it." The seed of an idea sprouts in my mind: I could call his mom, invite her here to celebrate the holiday with us, and give him the connection he's craving. I almost suggest it. But it feels too big, too presumptuous. Instead, I just say, "I'm glad you were there tonight."

"Me too."

We reach the cottage, and Dash beats me to the keypad. He opens the door, and I step inside and stop short just inside the door.

A Roman shade covers the big window behind the couch. It's gorgeous—creamy fabric with a subtle damask pattern, clean lines, clearly expensive.

"Where did this come from?"

Dash rubs the back of his neck. "I ordered it this morning. There's an interior design place in the valley that does rush orders. They delivered and installed it while we were at the tree farm."

I turn to stare at him. "You had a custom window treatment installed in one day?"

"I know you wanted privacy. Boundaries. After Shane's stunt …" he trails off, then starts over. "I heard you, Ivy. I want you to feel safe when you're with me."

My throat tightens. He spent money—probably a lot of money. Made phone calls. Coordinated with strangers. All to give me something I asked for.

"If you don't like it, they can take it down easily," he continues quickly. "They promised they'd repair any holes or damage when they remove it. The cottage will be exactly how it was before."

"It's beautiful," I say thickly.

"Yeah?" He looks relieved. "I wanted to make sure it was nice, not just functional. The designer texted me a bunch of options, and this one seemed like it would fit the cottage's style."

"It's perfect. Thank you." I mean it. But it feels off, wrong, like an itchy sweater or a shirt that shrunk in the wash.

"You take the bed tonight," he says.

"Dash—"

"I insist. I already put fresh sheets on and everything."

"But—"

"Please let me do this for you, after what you did for me today."

He's being thoughtful. Respectful. Giving me exactly what I asked for—space, boundaries, safety.

So why does my chest feel tight? Why do I want to tell him he's got it all wrong?

"Okay," I hear myself say as if someone else is talking. "Thank you."

He grins. "Good. I'm going to grab a pillow and claim the couch. Sweet dreams of mountain laurel."

"Good night."

He disappears into the bedroom and I follow him in, then veer into the bathroom and get ready for bed. Then I run the water until I hear him return to the living room and settle onto the couch. The sounds of him getting comfortable—rustling blankets, adjusting pillows—feel very far away.

I walk into the bedroom, close the door, and turn out the light. The bed is perfectly made, pillows fluffed, covers turned down. He even left a glass of water on the nightstand and switched on the bedside lamp.

I sink onto the edge of the mattress.

Everyone I love is taking risks. Making leaps. Choosing courage over caution.

Dash listened to me. Heard what I said I wanted. Gave it to me.

I asked for boundaries. He gave me a literal barrier.

This is what I wanted.

Isn't it?

I lie back on the too-perfect bed and stare at the ceiling.

Why does doing the right thing feel so wrong?

The bed's too cold without him beside me. I grab my fuzzy socks and sweatshirt and pull them on. But I'm still not comfortable. I sigh and roll to my side, then back to my back.

Azalea, black-eyed Susan, calla lily, daisy.

CHAPTER 16

A PUBLIC RELATIONS CAT-ASTROPHE

Dash

After a not-so-sensible breakfast of a thick slice of Merry's gingerbread apple coffee cake (washed down with my iced green drink as penance) and a quick shower, I leave the cottage and swing by Nick's workshop in the garage to pick up Ivy. She's sitting on a sawhorse table, keeping her father company as he runs a wood lathe over a piece of cedar. The small workspace smells like fresh pencil shavings.

Ivy catches my eye and waves. Nick turns off the lathe and pushes his safety glasses to the top of his head.

"Morning, Dash."

"Good morning," I reply. "Do you mind if I steal your daughter?"

"Just so long as you promise to return her," he cracks.

I wonder what it would have been like to grow up with a dad like Nick Jolly. I can't imagine it any more than I could imagine growing up at the North Pole, so I dismiss the thought.

Ivy hops off the table and kisses him on the cheek. And then we head out for my personal tour of Mistletoe Mountain. She's arranged for Farah, a college student looking for extra cash, to watch the flower shop for her today. So we have all day to wander.

She insists we start at the Snowflake Cafe, Delphina's coffee shop. When we walk inside a cloud of scent envelopes us. Cinnamon, cardamom, and gingerbread mingling with the aroma of strong coffee in a delicious, heady perfume. A vintage chandelier made entirely of Christmas ornaments catches the morning light, sending prisms across the pink and white tile floor.

Behind the counter, the espresso machine hisses steam. Jazzy instrumental holiday music plays over the speakers. We're early enough that we've beat the crowd of caffeine seekers Ivy says will descend on the shop over the next hour. We walk right up to the gleaming counter. A handful of early risers sit at the tables in front of the window, watching us with open interest while they sip their drinks and nibble on pastries.

Delphina spots us and her whole face lights up under her green elf hat. She leans across the counter and stage-whispers, "You two are trending."

"We're what?" Ivy asks, but Delphina's already spinning her tablet around.

Photos from yesterday's tree farm visit fill the screen. Me and Ivy by the bonfire, our heads close together. Her carrying the tree with her sisters. Me drinking cider while she smiles at something Jack is saying. The photos are perfect. The hashtags make me cringe, as usual: #DashAndIvy #SmallTownRomance #VampireGoesPastoral.

"Eighty-six thousand likes on this one already." Delphina taps a photo of Ivy brushing snow off my shoulder. "You two are adorable."

Through the frosted window, I spot the photographers who've been tailing us since we left the cottage approaching. Shane's already inside, pretending to study the pastry case with intense concentration. He's not fooling anyone.

"What can I get you?" Delphina asks.

I glance at the menu board, which features drinks with names like "Sugarplum Latte" and "Gingerbread Bliss." I'm in over my head.

"Whatever Ivy's having," I say.

Ivy grins. "You sure about that?"

"How bad could it be?"

Five minutes later, I'm staring at a to-go tumbler topped with what appears to be a cloud of pink foam studded with candy cane pieces.

"Is this a dessert?" I ask.

"Welcome to the holiday season at the Snowflake Cafe." Ivy laughs. "It's basically melted Christmas in a cup."

I take a cautious sip. Sugar explodes across my tongue,

followed by white chocolate and cream and peppermint. It's ridiculous. It's delicious. I'm a convert.

"Oh, before I forget!" Delphina leans forward conspiratorially. "Titus is doing the soft opening for his Cat Cafe today. He's been planning this for months—he'd be over the moon if you stop by. And bring your entourage." She gives a nod toward the press.

Ivy beams. "We will absolutely do that."

A chalkboard near the register catches my eye: "Suspended: 12 coffees, 8 meals." Below it, in smaller letters: "Pay it forward. Someone's always hungry."

"What's this about?" I ask, pointing.

"Oh, the suspended program? Anyone can buy an extra coffee or meal for someone who needs it. We don't make a big deal about it—folks just come in and ask if there's anything suspended, and we take care of them."

She says it like it's a small thing, but it's not. In LA, I write checks to charities for the tax deduction. Here, neighbors buy each other lunch.

"That's …," I start, but I don't have words for what it is.

"That's Mistletoe Mountain," Ivy finishes softly, and her hand finds mine.

Shane's camera clicks by the pastry case as I dig some bills out of my wallet, pass them to Delphina, and ask her to add to them to the kitty.

We take our sugary concoctions to go and head down the street to Frost & Fizz Soap Works. The small shop is tucked between a vintage clothing store and a yarn shop and is easy to miss if you're not looking for the baby blue front door.

The moment we step inside, yet another wall of layered scent hits me. This one is pine and peppermint and vanilla and cranberry, sugar and spice. Every surface is covered with colorful soaps, bath bombs, and lotions, all with handwritten labels and kraft paper packaging tied with twine bows.

Behind the counter, a woman with long silver hair in a thick braid looks up and smiles. Her apron is dusted with something sparkly—mica powder, maybe. "Ivy, so good to see you!"

"Hi, Autumn. This is—"

The woman laughs, "I know who Dash Pine is, girl." She grins at me, "I'm Autumn Frost. This is my shop. Look around. Let me know if you need anything."

I whisper to Ivy. "Is her name really—?"

"It really is."

I grin at the absurdity as I wander through the shop, picking up and sniffing the winter-themed bar soaps. Frostbitten Fir soap is dark green with silver swirls. There's also Mistletoe Kiss, pale green studded with what look like tiny white and red berries. Rust-colored Cinnamon Stick smells exactly like its name.

"Shopping for someone special?" Ivy asks, appearing at my elbow.

"My mom. She works hard. Doesn't really treat herself. Even now, when I have all the money in the world, she works like she thinks this will all disappear one day."

Ivy's expression softens and she presses her hand against my cheek. "It's sweet of you to treat her since she doesn't treat herself."

I don't know how to respond to this, so I take her hand and lift it to my mouth. As I drop a kiss on to her warm palm, the photographers crowded around the window outside the tiny store snap pictures in a frenzy.

I move to the next display and choose bath bombs that fizz silver and blue, body butter in a vintage-style tin labeled Northern Lights, and several foaming hand soaps named for the sweets from *The Nutcracker*.

When I bring my shopping basket up to the counter, Autumn compliments my choices as she rings up my purchases. "I can gift wrap and ship these for you," she offers. "I ship all over—had an order go to Dubai last week."

"That would be great."

I recite my mom's mailing address and phone number for Autumn. While I'm signing the credit card slip, I catch movement in my peripheral vision. Ivy's grabbed a pen from the counter and is scribbling something on her forearm, under her sweater sleeve. She catches me looking and smiles innocently.

I offer to take a picture with Autumn, and she practically leaps over the counter to stand beside me and smile as Ivy dutifully snaps a few shots with Autumn's cell phone.

"Okay if I post this on my social media?" Autumn asks.

"I'd be offended if you didn't," I tell her.

Once Ivy and I are back on the sidewalk I say, "What was that?"

"What was what?"

"You wrote something on your arm."

"Just a reminder." She won't meet my eyes, and I'm about to press when she gasps. "Oh! I almost forgot—look what Autumn gave me while you were shopping." She pulls a small glass jar from her coat pocket.

"What is it?"

"A sample of a new body scrub she's working on. Currently, she's calling it Reindeer Dust."

"What even is reindeer dust?"

"Sugar, coffee grounds, and holiday magic, which is what Autumn calls glitter."

Titus' Teahouse & Cat Cafe is a restored Victorian house with bay windows and a pressed tin ceiling that catches the afternoon light. The space is quirky, with mismatched vintage teacups, velvet furniture, loads of plants, and overloaded bookshelves. And more cats than I can count. Cats on climbing trees. Cats in window perches. Cats sleeping in sunbeams. Cats on shelves. Cats everywhere. Fur floats through the air and tumbles along the wood floor.

Titus bustles out from a back room to greet us. The bartender turned teahouse proprietor's nervous energy is palpable. I get it. This cafe is his dream made real, and there's a certain terror to that.

He embraces Ivy and then hits me with the classic bro handshake/one-armed hug. "Thanks for coming, man."

"We wouldn't miss it," I say as I slap his back and stifle a sneeze.

There's a small crowd of soft-opening attendees, including Shane. He's trying to blend in, but his camera and his smirk give him away.

Ivy makes a beeline for a Persian cat lounging on a window seat. She scoops it up, nuzzling its face.

"That's Lady Marmalade," Titus tells her.

"Isn't she a pretty kitty?" Ivy coos.

I'm not sure if she's talking to me or the feline. The cat is objectively gorgeous—long cream-colored fur, flat face, amber eyes. But my own eyes are already starting to water.

"Yeah, beautiful," I manage.

Two minutes later, my eyes are actively burning. I rub them furiously, which, of course, only makes it worse. Then my nose starts to run.

"You okay?" Ivy asks, still cuddling the cat.

"Fine. Probably."

I don't want to ruin Titus' opening. But my eyes are beginning to swell. I need to get out of here.

"Here, hold King Cole," Titus suggests, as he tries to place a black kitten with enormous yellow eyes in my arms. "I'm not really a cat person," I apologize, backing away.

I bump directly into Shane.

Click.

He catches the image of my red, watering eyes, refusing to hold the kitten as I grimace. And there's no doubt he heard me. Ivy's crestfallen expression confirms it.

"He's going to make you look like a monster."

I try to laugh it off. "I'm obviously allergic. That's not a crime." But even as I say it, I know Shane's going to sell the photo multiple times, and I'm already imagining the headlines. "Dash the Dog Trashes Cats" or "Bad Boy Dash Pine Can't Even Be Nice to Kittens" or something worse than anything I can come up with.

"We should go," Ivy says quietly.

Titus looks stricken, and I feel like I've ruined his opening, which makes the whole mess that much worse. I mumble an apology and stumble outside, where the cold air hits my face like salvation. I can breathe again. But a boulder of dread sits in my stomach.

CHAPTER 17

THE G.O.A.T.

Ivy

I've committed to doing something brave today, and I'm not about to let this cat situation derail me. So I pilot Dash down the hill to Rudy's Roadhouse on the edge of town, plotting my next moves. Rudy's is an after-midnight kind of place, and it's never busy during the day. By the time we've walked the length of town, his face is almost back to normal and he's stopped sneezing.

I push open the door and usher him inside. As expected, the bar is deserted. And as always, it smells like French fries and draft beer. I don't see a waiter anywhere, so I wave to the bartender and we seat ourselves, peanut shells crunching under our feet as we slide into a sticky booth. The walls are covered in vintage Mistletoe Mountain photos—the town square in the 1950s, the ski lodge being built, a summer parade with everyone in period costume.

The jukebox plays something twangy and mournful. Appropriate.

Rudy himself comes out from the back to take our order. Dash stares down at his phone, most likely watching the photo go live in real time, so I order for both of us. I keep it simple: two glasses of water and an order of poutine.

Rudy takes the laminated menu and leaves. Dash is still scrolling. His jaw gets tighter with each swipe.

"Comments?" I ask, although I don't really want to know.

"Mixed. Some people are calling it out as unfair. Others are ..." he trails off, but I can fill in the blank.

Others are gleeful. The mighty Dash Pine has fallen. Again. My heart aches for him. This is the exact spiral he came here to avoid.

"Will you be okay if I hit the ladies' room?"

He finally looks up, distracted. "What? Sure."

"You should wash your hands, too."

He gives me a blank expression. "Why?"

"Because you're obviously allergic to cat dander." I drop this truth bomb on him, slide out from the booth, and beeline to the restrooms before I lose my nerve.

Inside the ladies' room, my heart pounds as I pull out my phone and tap in the digits I scribbled on my arm when Dash recited them for Autumn. I lean against the wall and listen to Rachel Pine's phone ring on the other end, silently practicing what I'll say.

"This is Rachel Pine." She answers her phone in a business-like manner, the way Holly does.

"Hi, Ms. Pine. My name is Ivy Jolly. I'm ... I'm with Dash."

"Has something happened to him? Is he okay?"

Oh, Kris Kringle. She thinks he's hurt.

I hurry to reassure her. "He's fine! Better than fine. He's great. I'm calling because he's spending some time with me and my family in Mistletoe Mountain, and I thought you might like to join us for part of the holiday month."

There's a long, silence. Just as I'm about to ask if she's still there, she speaks.

"Dasher asked you to call?"

I chew on my lip. "Well, no. He doesn't know I'm calling. But he mentioned that you and he never really had a chance to celebrate Christmas together, and if there's one thing this town does well, it's celebrate."

Another pause. Then she says, "Where is this town of yours?"

Yes. I make a victorious fist and give her the broad strokes about Mistletoe Mountain. She tells me she'll text me her flight information, and I hang up feeling almost giddy. A surprise visit from his mom ought to cheer Dash up, regardless of what happens with the cat drama.

As I'm hurrying back to the booth, Griselda Alexander sweeps into the roadhouse like a tall, thin tornado in athletic shoes. I lock eyes with her and break into a full sprint. She still beats me to Dash.

Dash

I'm several pages deep into the online discourse about whether I hate all cats or, as an impassioned minority insists, have a fear of black cats. A poster with the handle VladDaddy4 is explaining this fear is called mavrogatphobia, and I'm wondering how that's pronounced when I glance up to see a tall, severe-looking woman marching straight toward me. She wears a velour sweatsuit and a scowl.

"I have an idea," she informs me as she takes Ivy's vacated spot, uninvited.

I eye her warily, trying to get a bead on her so I handle this the right way. The actual last thing I need right now is to get caught being snarky with a delusional fan. I casually scan the bar in search of any photographers trying to blend in with the nonexistent crowd.

"They're outside."

"Pardon?"

"The press. Well, the press and Shane Nottingham." Her voice is cool, almost bored.

"Do I know you?"

As I'm asking the question, Ivy races to the table. "This is Griselda Alexander," she pants.

The woman, Griselda, shoots her a withering look. "You wouldn't be out of breath right now if you didn't skip my Showstopper Cardio class on Wednesday mornings. And your pace would be better."

Ivy takes a deep breath before responding, "One, it took me so long because I got stuck in a puddle of a mystery substance that I am praying was gum. And two, you know I love that class. But it's hard to swing it while I'm trying to get my flower shop off the ground. I honestly don't always have the time."

Griselda's face softens and she scoots over to make room for Ivy.

I just stare at both of them until Ivy explains, "Griselda owns Maple Twist Fitness. Her classes are out of this world, but she *also* used to be a child star. Like you."

Griselda Alexander? I search every crevice of my brain and come up empty. "Sorry, I've never heard of you."

"I'm not surprised. My fame peaked before you were born. But I've done it all—appeared in Broadway musicals, had a recurring role as the precocious daughter of the married sleuths in a long-running detective comedy, and then danced on concert tours. So I know a thing or two about managing a public image."

I sit back. "Huh. Okay, what's your idea?"

She gives me a satisfied smile before answering, "Stillwater Animal Rescue has been kicking around the idea of doing a Santa Paws fundraiser to benefit the cats, dogs, and other animals in their sanctuary. Henry Stillwater was planning to wait until next year, get all his metaphorical and literal ducks in a row first—"

"The rescue has ducks?"

Ivy laughs lightly. "It's a sanctuary farm. It has everything. Cats, dogs, ducks, pigs, an adorable tripod goat."

"A three-legged goat?"

"Simone is the greatest."

Griselda grimaces at this detour from her plan. "But in light of recent events, Titus has offered the Cat Cafe as a venue this year. It would be damage control for him and good publicity for the rescue. Henry agreed."

"That sounds smart for both of them. I'm not sure how it helps me. I could write a check, I guess."

"No. You'll emcee the event."

I stare at her. "You want me to host a pet adoption event after I just went viral for hating cats?"

"You don't hate cats. You're allergic to them. There's a difference, and we're going to make sure everyone knows it." She's already typing on her phone. "We load you up on allergy meds and get photos of you with adoptable dogs, cats, even the goat. We turn this into an opportunity to highlight shelter needs. We control the narrative. And you and Titus both get the halo effect of supporting the cause."

It's not a bad plan. Actually, it's a good plan. Even Brody would like this plan. But I remain confused on one point.

"Why would you do this?" I ask. "Help me?"

She looks up from her phone, genuine surprise on her face. "We take care of our own here."

"But I'm not—" I start, then stop.

"Not what? Not from here?" She waves the idea away. "You're with Ivy. That's enough."

Under the table, Ivy finds my hand with hers and squeezes.

This is *not* how things work in Hollywood. I know better than anyone. In Hollywood, when you screw up, people distance themselves. Your agent stops returning calls. Your friends suddenly have other plans. Everyone waits to see if you'll survive before they decide whether to acknowledge they know you.

But here, in this quirky Christmas town, they stand together and problem solve. They care about each other. And, it seems, me.

My voice is rough with emotion when I say, "Let's do it. When?"

"Day after tomorrow. That gives us time to promote it and for you to get started on a course of allergy medication." Griselda's already texting someone. "I'll coordinate with the rescue and Titus. You just show up and be charming."

"I can do that," I promise. I'd better do it.

My phone buzzes. I glance down at the display. Brody's calling. No doubt he's seen the picture of Dash Pine, feline hater, and has some thoughts he'd like to share. I silence it.

For the first time since Shane snapped his photo, I can breathe.

"Thank you," I say to Griselda.

Griselda doesn't look up from her phone. "You're welcome. You're dismissed."

Ivy squeezes the woman's arm. "You're the best, Grizz. Love you."

She keeps her eyes glued to the screen but a small smile creeps over her face.

We settle up with Rudy for the congealed poutine fries and walk out into the late afternoon. The sun has begun to dip low, painting the snow pink and gold.

"So this is how Mistletoe Mountain operates, huh?"

"Call it the Mistletoe Mountain magic."

But this is more than that. This is Ivy's community. She's woven into the fabric of this place—knows everyone's names, remembers their stories, shows up when they need her. And by standing next to her, I'm being woven in, too.

The photographers' cameras click as they walk backward up the hill in front of us. But I'm not performing. I'm just walking alongside Ivy. Where I belong.

CHAPTER 18

SIMMERING

Ivy

Leave it to Griselda to enter from stage left with a viable solution to the cat disaster. Her timing, as always, is spot on. My shoulders unclench, and walking next to me, Dash stops checking his phone every seven seconds and stows it in his pocket on Do Not Disturb.

"Want to grab dinner?" he asks, hands still shoved in his coat pockets.

I can't. I need to go back to the flower shop. I should check on tomorrow's orders, respond to the seventeen texts from Merry, and prepare the supplies for my wreath-making workshop.

So why do I hear myself say, "Wanna cook instead?"

His eyebrows shoot up. "Cook? Like, actual cooking?"

"Mountain Organics is right there." I point across the square to the small storefront with its handwritten chalkboard signs visible through the window. "We could make soup. Bread. Something warm."

He studies my face for a moment, deliberating. Then he grins. "Okay. But I'm warning you—my kitchen skills peak at scrambling eggs. I definitely can't make bread."

"I'll bake the bread. Think you can handle chopping vegetables?"

"With sufficient direction, it shouldn't be any harder than rescuing a bag of flour from rising waters."

As we cross the square, snow crunching underfoot, I'm smiling so wide my face hurts. Or maybe that's frostbite.

Mountain Organics is busy, as usual. I grab a basket from the stack by the door and we navigate the narrow aisles lined with wooden bins and glass jars, everything labeled in neat handwriting. Behind the counter, Marcus Chen waves at us while bagging Marley Jacobs' groceries.

I toss produce into the basket—carrots, celery, onions, potatoes. I skip the herbs; Dad keeps the cottage stocked with spices. Dash trails behind me.

"They have it," he says, holding up a small tin of matcha powder.

"I told you we're not completely backward."

"I never said backward. I said charming." He adds the tin to our basket. "And maybe a little stuck in a snow globe."

"Fair."

At the register, Marcus rings us up while pretending not to stare at Dash. "Making dinner together? That's nice."

Dash slides his credit card across the counter. "First time for everything."

"Ivy's a good teacher." Marcus bags our items. "She taught my daughter how to arrange flowers last summer. Very patient, and she has a sneaky sense of humor, quiet as she is."

"I've noticed," Dash says warmly.

Flustered, I redirect their attention. "Caitlyn's a quick study. Do you want to get Dash's autograph for her? Or a picture?"

"For her? How about for me?" Marcus laughs.

Dash waves him around the counter and I snap a handful of shots with Marcus' phone. Maybe I should add photographer to my resume. The thought makes me snicker, and it hits me that we haven't seen the photographers since before Rudy's.

I mention this to Dash after we leave the warmth of the market.

He nods. "They're probably stoking the fires of the #DashVsCats drama by reposting old shots of me behaving less than perfectly and updating the stories about us. The internet moves fast; they have to milk the story while they can."

His matter-of-fact delivery doesn't fool me. He's still beating himself up.

"An allergy isn't a character flaw," I remind him. "And

once Griselda announces the Santa Paws fundraiser, you'll be the good guy again."

"I know. Everything's cyclical in the entertainment business. Sometimes, though, I feel like a hamster on a wheel."

He's the hottest hamster I've ever seen, but I keep this thought to myself. We walk the rest of the way to the cottage in comfortable silence, swinging our bags of groceries between us.

Inside the cottage, I kick off my boots and put the bags down in the kitchen while Dash shrugs out of his coat.

He pulls out his phone. "Music?"

"Sure. Nothing too Christmassy, please. It's a long month of holiday music around here."

Acoustic coffeehouse music fills the cottage.

"How's this?"

"Perfect."

I tie my hair back and wash my hands while Dash rolls up his sleeves. I'm acutely aware of sharing the small kitchen space with him.

I pull out a large glass bowl. "Bread first. It needs time to rise."

"I've never made bread. I've never *met* anybody who makes bread."

"It's easier than you think. And therapeutic." I measure flour into the bowl, then hand him the measuring cup. "Your turn. Two more cups, then a quarter cup more."

He's quiet, concentrating as he levels each cup with the

back of a knife. I add the yeast and salt and whisk the ingredients together then pour in the warm water.

I give him a spatula.

"What do I do with this?"

"Mix it around until it forms a sticky ball."

He shoots me a skeptical look but does it. When the dough takes shape, he gives an excited shout and I try to hide my amusement.

"Now what?"

"Now we cover the bowl and wait."

"Wait for what?"

"For it to rise. It'll take at least two hours, maybe more. We want it to double in size. We can make the soup in the mean time."

The playlist ends. "More music?" He reaches for his phone.

"Sure or a podcast." I glance at him. "Or we could talk."

"What would we talk about?"

"I don't know. Normal people things. Favorite foods. Memorable cooking disasters. Whatever."

He laughs. "Okay, we'll give it a try."

I stretch one of the reusable covers that Merry swears by over the bowl and set the dough aside. He uncorks a bottle of red wine and pours us each a glass, then studies the vegetables on the counter. "Where do we start?"

"Chopping. I'll show you."

I show him how to hold a knife and move his hand while we chop the first carrot. Then I push the rest of the carrots toward him. "You do the rest."

Again, he follows my instructions carefully.

I peel the onions and add them to his pile. "Cut these in quarters and then dice them."

"Yes, chef."

He attacks them with gusto, but tears start streaming down his face, he gives me a look as though I've betrayed him.

"You didn't warn me about this."

"Try breathing through your mouth."

He does. "That doesn't help."

"No, but it's what everyone says to do."

He laughs through the tears, wiping his eyes with his sleeve. "You're enjoying this."

"A bit." I bump his hip with mine, surprising us both. "But you're doing great. Look at your perfect dice."

He works his way through the vegetables—more carrots, celery, potatoes. Dash gets faster and more confident. I sauté the aromatics in an enamel Dutch oven while he continues chopping. Before long, the kitchen fills with the sweet scent of caramelizing onions and garlic.

"Brody called this afternoon," Dash says suddenly, the knife stilling.

"Oh? About the cat situation?"

"No. He called with a job offer." He doesn't look at me and returns to dicing potatoes with careful precision.

"Congratulations."

"Maybe. We'll see."

I sip my wine and wait, but he doesn't elaborate. So I don't push.

"If you don't cook, do you order takeout every night? Or go out to eat?"

He gives me a sheepish look. "I have a chef."

Of course he has a personal chef. Somehow, I managed to forget briefly that he's not a regular person. He's rich. He's famous. He's Dash Pine.

"Vegetables are done," he announces.

I dump them into the pot, add the vegetable stock, seasonings, and a generous splash of wine. I cover the pot and leave the soup to simmer.

"More waiting," I tell him.

I wash the dishes and wipe down the counters while he lights a fire. I carry our wineglasses into the living room and we claim opposite ends of the couch. The soup simmers. The bread rises. The fire crackles. Quiet domesticity with the sexiest man alive—literally.

"I've never sat around waiting for bread to bake. It's relaxing."

"It's not a regular hobby for me either," I tell him. "Even since I opened Blooms, I've been working like a Wall Street finance bro. Always hustling, pulling all-nighters. I slept at the shop a few times."

"You're smiling about it, though," he observes.

"I love what I do," I say simply.

"I get it. It's how I feel—felt—about acting. An eighteen-hour day on set used to get me pumped up."

"Not anymore, though?"

He frowns into his wineglass. Finally he says, "At some point, I guess I started to feel disconnected from that excitement. The Cody Jones role was supposed to bring that spark back …." He trails off.

The fire pops. He turns toward the hearth and then stands abruptly. "I'm going to get more firewood."

The fire's fine. We don't need more wood. But I let him escape the conversation.

After the door closes behind him, I check my phone. I have a text from his mom:

> All set. I got a seat on the red-eye. I land in Burlington at 10 am tomorrow. Don't tell Dasher. Let's surprise him.

My thumbs fly:

> Perfect. I'll pick you up in the morning. Safe travels!

I grin, my heart full at the idea of bringing Dash and his mom together for a real Christmas celebration, even if it'll be an early one. The door bursts open and cold air rushes in. I shove my phone into my pocket.

Dash hurries inside, his arms full of firewood, snowflakes dusting his dark hair and unfairly long eyelashes.

"It's snowing!" He dumps the wood beside the hearth.

"It's December in Vermont, Dash. It's always snowing."

"Not like this. Come see." He pulls me to my feet and tosses my parka at me.

I put on the coat and my boots and follow him outside. He's right; this isn't regular snow. It's the kind of snowfall you see in the movies. Fat flakes tumble from the sky. Falling rapidly, they blanket the ground in pristine white.

I bend down and scoop up a handful. I pack it loosely. "Have you ever had a snowball fight?"

"In Southern California? Uh, no."

I lob my snowball gently. It hits his shoulder.

"I see how it is," he says, dusting the snow from his shoulder and forming a snowball of his own. He throws it like it's a football. It smacks me directly in the face, then explodes, sending snow cascading down my shoulder.

The cold stings my skin, and I stand there, stunned for a moment.

He runs over. "I'm so sorry. I was aiming for your shoulder, I swear. Are you okay?"

He reaches out and gently brushes the snow from my face. His fingers are warm on my frozen cheeks. His dark eyes search mine, worried. A cloud of warm air leaves his mouth each time he breathes. He's so close I can feel his breath on my lips.

Too close.

I grab a handful of the snow from my coat sleeve and shove it down the back of his collar.

He yelps, and I'm already running, squealing, slipping in the snow as I race toward the cottage. His footsteps pound behind me, closer, closer—

I make it to the porch steps just as his arm wraps around my waist, spinning me around. We're both laughing, both breathless, both covered in snow. His arm still encircles me. I press my palm against his chest and feel the rapid beat of his heart. Snow swirls around us.

The cold air is charged with electricity, possibility. Neither of us moves.

Finally, I shiver and pull away, heading back inside before I say or do something I can't take back.

"Mind if I take a hot shower?" he rasps.

I don't trust myself to talk, so I shake my head. He heads into the bathroom, and I trade my wet clothes for cozy pajama bottoms and soft tee. While he showers, I make the bread. I definitely do not think about him naked, just feet away, as I shape the dough into a round loaf, score it, and slide it into the preheated oven. Not at all.

He returns to the kitchen wearing dry clothes, his hair damp and his face flushed from the heat of the shower, just as the timer goes off. The bread is perfect, golden-brown and crusty. The soup is fragrant and ready. We ladle the soup into bowls, slice the bread, and refill our glasses.

We eat at the island.

"We made this," Dash says, amazed. "And it's good."

"It really is." I tear off a piece of bread and pop it into my mouth. "You're a natural."

"I had a good teacher."

After we eat, we clean up together—him washing, me drying, moving around each other like dancers. By unspoken agreement we head back to the living room with the wine.

"Movie?" I suggest. "*Miracle on 34th Street* is on."

"I've never seen it."

"How is that possible? It's a classic."

"Let's do it."

We settle on the couch. The flames in the fireplace dance, casting shadows on the wall. The drawn Roman shade cocoons us in privacy. I pull a warm blanket down from the back of the couch and drape it over us as the movie starts.

I don't decide to lean against him. It just happens. One minute I'm sitting upright, cradling my wineglass, and the next, my head rests on his shoulder. Then, somehow, I'm tucked against his side, his arm around me, my ear pressed to his chest.

His hand traces idle circles on my shoulder. His heartbeat thuds in my ear. The movie plays.

I should say goodnight and go to the bedroom, I think hazily.

Instead, my heavy eyelids close over my eyes and I sigh contentedly.

I wake to movement. I'm being lifted by strong arms under me, nestled against warm skin.

I make a small sound of protest but don't open my eyes.

"Shh," Dash murmurs. "I've got you."

I relax against him as he carries me to the bedroom.

He places me gently on the bed and pulls the covers over me. I sink into the mattress, still half-asleep. The covers are soft underneath me. I hear him step back.

Take a risk.

I open my eyes and reach out to catch his hand. "Stay."

He freezes. "Ivy—"

"Stay," I repeat. "Please."

"You're sure?"

I pull back the covers beside me and move over to make room. "I'm sure."

He joins me with a rustle of sheets and blankets and wraps his arm around my waist, tugging me close, my back against his chest. I lace my fingers through his where they rest on my stomach.

I murmur, "Goodnight."

He presses his mouth to my ear. "Goodnight, Ivy."

My breathing slows and I drift back to sleep without naming a single flower.

CHAPTER 19

STAYING

Dash

I wake to the weight of Ivy's leg thrown over mine, her hand splayed on my chest, her breath warm against my neck. The first time she woke up snuggled next to me, she practically launched herself across the room. This morning, she's draped over me like I'm her personal body pillow. It's a role I'm happy to play.

Pale winter light filters through the sheer curtains. The cottage is quiet except for her steady breathing and the occasional creak of the old building settling. I should get up—make coffee, check my phone, do something productive.

Instead, I smooth her vanilla-scented hair back from her face and memorize the constellation of freckles on her cheeks, the rise and fall of her ribs with her breath, the small sleepy sound she makes when I shift slightly.

She stirs, sighs, and curls her fingers into the fabric of my shirt.

"Morning," I murmur.

She goes still for a moment. I hold my breath for that split second of reorienting while she remembers where she is and who she's with. Then she relaxes and burrows closer.

"Too early," she mumbles.

I smile at the ceiling. "Want me to get up and make coffee?"

"No." She clamps her hand down on my chest as if she could pin me in place. "Stay."

"I'm not going anywhere," I promise. "Except the kitchen."

She tilts her head up, blinking sleep-glazed eyes at me, her hair a wild tangle. "Coffee in bed?"

"You've got it. Or I could make you one of my matcha abominations if you want. Someone has to save you from your sugar addiction."

"My sugar addiction is what makes me delightful." She gives me a playful push. "Coffee in bed sounds perfect. As long as it's actual coffee."

"Deal."

I ease out from under her carefully and hurry to the kitchen, the floor cold under my bare feet.

When I return with two mugs—hers with sugar, mine

black—she's propped up against the pillows and her hair is in a messy knot on the top of her head.

I hand her the candy-cane striped mug and sit on the edge of the bed.

She takes a sip and sighs happily. Then she turns her green eyes my way. "What's on your agenda today?"

"I'm meeting Griselda at her fitness studio. She's giving me a lift to our nine o'clock meeting with Titus and Henry at the animal rescue. We're going to finalize the Santa Paws plans and make sure I know which animals to avoid if I want my face to remain normal-sized."

She laughs. "All of them, probably."

"I'll take the meds. I'll be fine." I bump her shoulder with mine. "What about you?"

"I need to talk to my sisters. Then I have some errands to run." She shifts her gaze away from mine.

"Errands?"

"Exciting stuff. Post office. Bank. You know. Adulting."

She's not telling me the whole truth. But I don't push. If she wants to tell me, she will.

"When should we meet up?"

"Let's plan to meet at the library Bookmas party this afternoon. And after that, there's Christmas karaoke at the Tipsy Turnip."

"Sure, that all sounds like fun."

"It will be," she promises. "And both events will be packed, so the photographers will be able to get some great shots."

I put my mug down on the nightstand and turn to her. "That's not why I want to go with you."

She blinks at me. "I don't understand."

"I'm staying. Or, at least, I want to stay."

She goes very still. "What?"

"After the week is up. I want to stay in Mistletoe Mountain." I hold her gaze. "I want to experience Christmas here. With you. If that's okay."

Her eyes go wide and impossibly green. For a terrible moment, she says nothing.

Then she sets her mug next to mine with deliberate care, turns to face me fully, and crawls into my lap.

My mouth finds hers and we kiss. Not a staged kiss. Not a kiss for the cameras. A kiss just for us. Her hands cradle my face. Mine are tangled in her hair.

When she pulls back, she's grinning.

"Is that a yes?" I tease.

"That's a heck yeah."

She's still smiling when she settles back against the pillows, reaching for her coffee again. But her hand is shaking slightly.

"Through Christmas," she says, trying for casual. "That's ... what, three weeks from now?"

"Give or take."

"And you'll stay here? At the cottage?"

"If that's okay." I pause. "Your dad told Brody it was available all month, so I think I can extend the reservation. You can stay here with me. But if you need to get back to your regular life—"

"No." She cuts me off. "I mean, I can stay here longer."

My chest expands. "Okay then."

We grin at each other like idiots until she clears her throat.

"We should probably get moving. I need to shower, and you have your meeting."

"Right. Adulting."

She slides out of bed and heads to the bathroom, taking her mug with her. A moment later, I hear the shower running. I flop back against the pillows, grab my phone, and thumb out a text to Brody letting him know the new plan.

By eight, we're both showered and dressed. When we leave the cottage together, the photographers are waiting, cameras ready, along the walkway that leads to the street. We're heading in different directions, so they're perfectly positioned to capture our goodbye kiss at the corner. We make it a good one—for us, and for them.

I watch her walk away before turning the opposite way.

I'm halfway to Maple Twist Fitness when I realize I'm humming. Actually humming. Like a cartoon character about to break into song. I should be embarrassed. Instead, I can't stop smiling.

A couple of the photographers trail behind me. I wonder if they can hear me humming.

Outside Mountain Organics, a woman with a toddler on her hip does a double-take. "You're Dash Pine!"

"Guilty," I say, expecting the usual photo request.

Instead she says, "I'm Samara. My daughter Evie helps

Ivy with deliveries sometimes." She waves the little boy's mittened hand, then shifts him to her other hip. "And this is Jalen."

"Hi, Jalen."

"Well, welcome to Mistletoe Mountain. And thanks for doing the Santa Paws thing. The Stillwaters do so much good for those rescued animals. I'm excited for the fundraiser."

"It's nice to meet you, Samara."

She grins and continues past me. No photo or autograph request, no fawning.

At the corner, I pause to let a group of elementary school kids cross. They're in a line, holding a jingle-bell-festooned length of rope. One kid—maybe six or seven years old—tugs her teacher's sleeve and points at me, whispering.

The teacher glances over, smiles, and keeps walking.

No interruption. No scene.

In Los Angeles, where you can't swing a cat without hitting a celebrity (although I would **never**, I've learned my lesson where cats are concerned), I've been ambushed everywhere, including my dentist's office while my teeth were actively being cleaned.

Here, though, even though people recognize me, they treat me like Ivy's boyfriend. A part of the town. I haven't been treated like a regular person in over a decade, since before I blew up as Vlad. To me, these ordinary interactions feel extraordinary.

Something about it makes me want to call Mom. I pull

out my phone, then stop. What would I even say? Hi, Mom. I'm having a fake relationship with a small-town florist but I think I'm falling for her for real. In fact, I want to spend Christmas in Vermont instead of taking the meetings Brody's setting up.

Yeah, that'll go over great.

We don't have that kind of relationship. We never have. She's my manager's second-in-command, my logistics coordinator. She's proud of my success because it justifies her sacrifices. She loves me and I love her. But we don't do heart-to-hearts.

There's nothing to tell her yet. Not really. Maybe after Christmas. Once I've figured out what this thing with Ivy actually is.

I shove the phone back in my pocket and wave to Griselda through the window of her fitness studio.

CHAPTER 20

ENTER RACHEL

Ivy

For the first part of my two-hour drive to Burlington, I call my sisters and arrange for Holly and Jack to take my room at the house Merry and I share, leaving Holly's loft free for Dash's mom. In exchange, they extract the details of my evening in with Dash. After they register their disappointment that all we did in bed was sleep, I end our conference call in a hurry.

I spend the rest of the drive rehearsing what I'll say when I meet Rachel Pine. But when she spots my white coat and walks toward me in the baggage claim area, my mind goes blank. She's taller than me, with Dash's dark eyes, long lashes, and defined bones, and she looks too young to have a son in his twenties. She also looks unfairly put together and refreshed for someone who just stepped off an overnight flight.

"Ms. Pine. Rachel. I'm Ivy. How was your flight? Hi."

She smiles indulgently at my babbling, then says, "Please call me Rachel. I'm so happy to meet you, Ivy. Can I give you a hug? I'm a hugger."

She swoops in for an embrace without waiting for an answer. The quick hug calms my nerves and slows my racing thoughts. I feel competent to form words by the time she steps back, still squeezing my shoulders, and studies me.

"You're even prettier than you look in pictures."

"Oh, you saw those?" I hope she didn't catch wind of the feline drama.

"I spent some time scrolling when I was waiting to depart LAX. You two have certainly caught the public's eye."

I blush, because of course I do. Then I reach for her carry-on. "Did you check a bag?"

"No. I travel light."

She follows me to the parking garage, asking polite questions about the drive, the weather, Vermont in December. Safe topics. But once we're on the highway heading south, the real questions start.

"So." She adjusts her seatbelt and turns to face me. "Tell me about Mistletoe Mountain."

I do. I tell her about the town square, the quirky shops, the Christmas traditions that run all month. The way everyone knows everyone. The suspended coffee program at the Snowflake Cafe. The banned books bingo at the library. And I tell her all about my family's inn.

"It sounds charming," she says. "Very different from Los Angeles."

"It is."

"You've been?"

"A few times. My cousin Rosemary lives out there."

"Tell me how you two met."

It's an innocent question. Of course, she wants to know how we met. So I tell her about the photo shoot, the flowers, how he helped me move a heavy planter. I don't mention Lia Campbell or the fake dating arrangement. That part doesn't matter anymore.

She's quiet for a long moment. When she speaks again, her voice is different. Careful. "You seem to have become quite serious, quite fast. He never mentioned you, and suddenly you're calling me and inviting me to visit."

"I don't know how serious we are," I admit. "But he told me you and he never had a big Christmas celebration. So when he decided to stay and experience Christmas in Mistletoe Mountain, I wanted to give him—give both of you—a family Christmas."

"With your family."

I glance away from the road and meet her eyes. "And you," I point out.

"And me."

"Rachel, I didn't mean to overstep. I only want Dash to be happy."

"And you think you this will make him happy?

Spending the holiday in a small town with you rather than going on one of our trips—Christmas in Maui or New Year's in Rio de Janeiro?"

There's no malice in her voice. But the implication is clear: I don't know him as well as she does.

"I think he's happy here," I say carefully. "I think he's found something he's been missing."

"Hmm." She turns to look out the window at the snow-capped mountains. "We'll see."

I turn on the radio hoping Christmas music will lighten both our moods. She hums along to a few songs and taps her fingers on her thigh in time to the music.

"If you like Christmas music, you should join us tonight," I tell her. "One of the restaurants, the Tipsy Turnip, hosts a karaoke night each year. This year, they expect an even bigger crowd than usual."

She gives me a genuine smile. "That sounds like great fun."

My worry fades. This is going to be fine. She's protective, that's all. That's normal for a mother, especially one who raised her son as a single mom.

When we reach the heart of Mistletoe Mountain and she sees the vintage storefronts, the twinkling lights strung everywhere, and Santa holding court in his gazebo, she actually claps her hands.

"It's like something out of a storybook—or a Hallmark movie!"

"Wait until you see the library," I tell her. Aside from the inn, it's my favorite building in town.

CHAPTER 21

VAMPIRE FOOD

Ivy

The library is a stone building that looks like it's been here since Vermont was founded, and probably has. Inside, the main reading room is dominated by a massive Christmas tree, and the air smells like old books and pine with a hint of jasmine tea wafting from the reference desk.

It's packed—kids, parents, townspeople milling around tables covered in craft supplies and wrapped books.

"Oh, look at the snowflake chains," Rachel breathes, taking it all in. "And the tree!"

"There's Dash." I point toward the children's wing.

Through a wall of glass, Dash is visible, perched on a stool and surrounded by kids on beanbags shaped like snowballs. He's reading aloud, doing different voices—gruff, squeaky, thunderous—completely unselfconscious.

She watches him for a long moment, and something complicated crosses her face. Pride mixed with something else I can't quite read. "He's so natural with them. I didn't know he was good with children."

"I don't know how he got roped into helping with story time, but he seems to be having fun. Come on, I'll introduce you to Noelle."

She looks back at Dash one last time before she follows me to the circulation desk, where we find Noelle helping two little boys thread hooks onto colorful ornaments.

"Okay, you two, go hang your ornaments on the tree."

"No storytime for them?" I ask as they race through the crowd, bobbing and weaving at top speed.

"I couldn't do that to Dash. The Williams twins are *very* active learners. They went up to the Wonder Workshop and 3D printed ornaments instead." She comes around the desk to greet us.

"Rachel, this is Noelle Winters, our library director and my dad's fian—wife."

Noelle laughs warmly. "We'll all get used to it eventually. It's so nice to meet you, Rachel. Welcome to Mistletoe Mountain."

"It's lovely to meet you."

"Dash didn't tell me he was doing story hour."

"He didn't know," Noelle says with a grin. "Jack sprang it on him at the last minute. Apparently a lot of the kids know who he is and are very excited that he's the guest reader."

Rachel nods. "That makes sense. *The Vampire Quarterback* is streaming now. There's a whole new generation of Vlad Graves fans."

"Let's catch the end of Dash's dramatic reading of *And Tango Makes Three*," Noelle suggests, leading us toward the hallway to the children's wing.

"Wait, that's a board book. Preschoolers aren't watching *The Vampire Quarterback*. Are they?"

Rachel shrugs, and Noelle grins. "There may be more older siblings than usual sitting in on this one."

I suddenly wonder how many preteens currently have posters of Dash plastered on their bedroom walls? I decide I don't want to know.

When we reach the doorway of the children's reading room, Evie Robinson spots me and nearly dumps her little brother Jalen off her lap and onto the floor in her excitement. "Ivy's here!"

"Looks like Dasher isn't the only celebrity around here," Rachel observes.

Dash waves me over. "Hey, Ivy! Come say hi to everyone." He's giving me that crooked smile that makes my stomach flip.

"Hi, friends," I say brightly, stepping into the room. I can sense Rachel following behind me. The photographers stationed near the door start snapping pictures.

His gaze shifts past me and his smile freezes.

"Mom?"

Rachel steps forward with her hands stretched out wide. "Surprise, sweetheart!"

For a moment, nobody moves. The kids stare. The parents stare. From just inside the doorway, Noelle stares. The photographers' cameras click rapid-fire.

Finally, Dash stands, setting the book aside carefully, and crosses the room to his mother. They hug, laughing, and I relax my tense shoulders.

"What are you doing here?"

"Ivy invited me." Rachel's smiling, but her eyes are alert, taking in the cameras and the watching crowd.

Dash turns to me. "You called my mom?"

I can't read his expression.

I nod, suddenly uncertain again. "To surprise you. You said you never had a real Christmas together, and there's nothing more real than a Mistletoe Mountain Christmas."

"She's so sweet, Dasher," Rachel enthuses.

Dash opens his mouth, but before he can respond, Caitlyn Chen tugs on his sleeve. Uh-oh.

"Is your mom a vampire, too?"

His laugh sounds genuine. "No, she's not."

A boy calls out, "What about Ivy?"

I turn toward the kids, grateful for the interruption. "What about me?"

Caitlyn picks up the baton. "Are you his girlfriend? Does that make you a vampire, too?"

I give Dash a panicked look. What should I say?

He extricates his arm from his mother's and comes over

to me, wrapping me in a hug from behind. "She is my girl-friend, but she's not a vampire."

Sunny Min, yet another precocious miniature citizen of Mistletoe Mountain, studies me, her tiny hands in fists on her hips. "That's because she's vampire food."

"Excuse me? Do I *look* like vampire food, Sunny?"

She nods seriously. "You're very pale."

Everyone laughs, and I lean back against Dash. For a moment, it's just us, sharing this ridiculous, perfect moment.

Then I remember it's not just us. I look over at Rachel. She's watching us intently.

Dash releases me from his arms and addresses the kids. "Well, that was exciting. But who wants me to finish the story?"

Enthusiastic shouts of "Me!" ring out.

He glances at Rachel, then me. "Give me a few minutes?"

"Of course," his mom says.

We rejoin Noelle near the doorway, and the three of us watch Dash engage the kids, several of whom are doubled over with laughter. I glance up to the catwalk outside the makerspace and see the Williams twins, listening from afar while also climbing a bookshelf. I elbow Noelle and point, and she rushes off to rescue them—or her books, more likely.

Rachel's expression is unreadable as she watches her son surrounded by giggling, rapt children.

"He's different here," she says quietly, more to herself than me.

"I think he can relax here," I tell her.

She looks at me with something—worry, or maybe fear—shadowing her expression. Whatever she might have said next is lost when the kids erupt in applause. Story hour is over.

The kids swarm Dash as he makes his way toward us. He's patient, asking their names, making jokes. He even does his Vlad voice for them.

Finally, he extracts himself and comes over to us.

"Sorry about that." He's smiling, but I can see the uncertainty in his eyes when he glances at his mother.

There's a beat of awkward silence. Dash is looking at me like he wants to say something. I'm trying to figure out what's wrong with Rachel. And Rachel is studying both of us like we're a puzzle she can't solve.

"Ivy," Rachel says suddenly, "would you mind if I borrow Dasher for a bit? I'd love to see more of the town. Just the two of us. We haven't had much time alone since he started splitting his time between Los Angeles and New York."

She says it sweetly. So sweetly that saying no would seem cruel.

Dash glances at me. I see the apology in his eyes, but also the ask. She's his mother. She came all this way.

"Of course," I hear myself say. "I should check on the flower shop anyway. Dash can get you settled in at the loft. I'll see you both later?"

"Tonight at Christmas karaoke," Dash promises. "The Tipsy Turnip. Seven o'clock."

"I'll be there." I stretch up onto my toes to give him a quick kiss and press my key chain into his hand so he can take my car and get his mom settled in at Holly's.

Then I turn to Rachel. "I'm so glad you're here."

"Thank you for inviting me, Ivy." Her voice is genuine and her face is open, kind.

As I leave, I glance back. Rachel's already steering Dash toward the exit, her hand on his arm, talking rapidly. He's listening, nodding.

And somehow, for a reason I can't pinpoint, it feels like it was a mistake to bring her here.

Outside, the cold air stings my face but doesn't ease my anxiety. I stand on the library steps, watching people come and go, trying to shake the uneasy feeling in my gut. After a few minutes, it's clear that feeling isn't going anywhere. I pull up my hood and head to the flower shop.

CHAPTER 22

NOT MOM'S CUP OF TEA

Dash

Mom wants to see the town.

It's a reasonable request. So I walk her through the square, pointing out the Snowflake Cafe, Frost & Fizz, Mountain Organics. She asks questions about everything—genuinely engaged, admiring the window displays, commenting on the charm of it all. I'm glad she's enjoying herself and happy to be spending this relaxed time with her.

But every time I try to steer us toward the inn, she finds another shop to explore. Another story to tell about when I was little. Another reason to delay.

"We should grab dinner," she says as the sun starts to

set. "Just us. We never get time alone anymore, and I want to hear everything. How you've really been."

I check my phone. Ivy hasn't texted. "Okay. But I'm supposed to meet Ivy at seven for—"

"Seven? Perfect. That gives us plenty of time." She links her arm through mine, and I give in.

After Vlad the vampire became a teen heart throb, our relationship shifted. She became a trusted advisor, a steady hand as I navigated fame. But this part—quiet mother/son time—was edged out, pushed to the side. I want to enjoy it now. So we head to dinner.

But we don't have plenty of time. By the time we finish "a quick bite" at the Sushi Station, it's 7:15. Mom shifts into business mode, telling me about a conversation she had with Brody, about the projects coming up, about how proud she is. Then she orders dessert. And coffee. By the time we reach the Tipsy Turnip, it's nearly eight.

I feel guilty about being late, but Mom seems so happy. So relaxed. I can't remember the last time I saw her this way.

The Tipsy Turnip is packed wall-to-wall when we finally arrive. Someone's butchering "Jingle Bell Rock" on the karaoke stage while the crowd cheers them on.

I scan the room for Ivy. She's at a high-top table near the back with her sisters, Quinn, and Delphina. When our eyes meet, she gives me a small wave. I wave back, hoping she'll come over, but she's deep in a conversation with Merry.

I'm about to suggest we head to Ivy's table when

Griselda introduces herself. "Hi, you must be Dash's mom. I'm Griselda Alexander." She gestures to the shorter, curvier woman beside her. "And this is my partner, Marley Jacobs."

Mom's eyes widen. "Not *the* Griselda Alexander who appeared in *Annie* and *Matilda* on Broadway?"

Griselda smiles, pleased. "The very same."

"I saw you in *Annie*! You were incredible." Mom's face lights up. "Honey, did you know—?"

"Actually, Mom, I need to talk to Ivy for a minute."

"Oh, of course! Go, go." She waves me off, already turning back to Griselda. "Tell me, are you still performing?"

I make it exactly three steps before Mom calls out, "Dasher! Would you get a drink with me first before you run off? I'm parched. And I want to hear all about Griselda's career."

I pause, torn. Ivy's right there. But Mom's genuinely excited—talking to Griselda about theater, about the life she gave up. How can I say no to that?

"Sure. Just a quick one."

It takes a while to fight our way to the bar. Titus stops us to tell Mom about the Cat Cafe. Autumn Frost pulls us aside to say she'll drop off my mom's gift tomorrow since she hasn't been to the post office yet. Everyone wants to meet my mother, and she's gracious with all of them— asking questions, remembering names.

When we finally reach the bar, I order a Frosty IPA for me and a candy cane martini for her. I spot Ivy at the other end of the bar, carrying a steaming mug. I call her name, and she turns to flash me a smile.

I pass my mom her martini and slip away to catch up with Ivy.

"Hot toddy?" I gesture toward her drink.

"Tea with lemon and honey. For Holly."

"Is she sick?"

She laughs. "No, she's being competitive. She saw Griselda and Marley drinking it earlier—vocal prep—and said she needed to up her game. She's in the ladies' room right now doing warm-ups."

We both laugh and I'm about to pull her close when my mom appears beside us.

"Ivy, what's that?" She nods at the mug, curious.

"Herbal tea," Ivy tells her.

"Oh." Mom pauses, something flickering across her face. "That's very mindful."

"Um, I guess?" Ivy gives me a confused look.

There's an awkward beat. Then Mom brightens. "Ivy, thank you again for inviting me. This town is delightful."

"I'm so glad you're here," Ivy says, but I can hear the uncertainty in her voice.

"I'd love to do a duet later," I tell Ivy, trying to bridge the weird moment. "Want to go pick something out?"

"Oh, but you have to sing with me first!" Mom exclaims. "Come on, Dasher. Just one song. I haven't sung in years. Not since—" she stops herself. "Well. It's been a long time."

The unspoken ending hangs there: Not since I gave up performing to raise you.

I glance at Ivy, apologetic. She gives me a tight smile. "Go on, sing with your mom. We'll do ours later."

Mom's already heading to Nebula's table to sign us up.

An hour later, I've sung two duets with my mother (she's fantastic, of course—the whole bar loved her), met approximately two dozen new people, and haven't had a single real conversation with Ivy.

Every time I try to make my way to her table, something happens. A tourist asks for a photo. Titus wants to confirm Santa Paws details. Mom needs another drink. Or she's in the middle of a conversation and gestures me over to introduce me.

I'm sure my mother's not doing it on purpose. She's just here. Present. And everyone wants to talk to her.

As if I've summoned her with the thought, she appears at my elbow. "This town really commits to the season, doesn't it?" She's smiling, but there's something wistful in her voice. "It's charming. Very ... settled."

I give her a close look. "You okay?"

"I'm fine." She glances toward Ivy, who's laughing with Quinn. "Your girlfriend is lovely. She fits in here perfectly."

"She does."

Mom's quiet for a moment. Then, carefully, "Do you?"

"Do I what?"

"Fit in here." She says it gently. "I'm just trying to understand, honey. This is so different from your life in LA. Do they have theater here? Museums? Culture? The things you're used to?"

"There's a theater in Stonebridge. And Manhattan's not that far." Why is she asking these questions?

"Of course." She touches my arm. "I'm not criticizing." A pause. "I want you to be happy. You know that, right?"

"I know."

"I just worry." She looks down at her drink. "I can tell you care about Ivy. But you've worked hard to get where you are. You need to remember that."

Before I can respond, Nebula calls my name. Just mine this time.

I look at Mom, confused. "I didn't sign up for a solo."

Griselda materializes beside us, grinning. "I did. Surprise! I picked something special. Trust me, you'll love it."

"Hope I know it."

"Everybody knows it."

The opening notes start as I take the mic, and I recognize it immediately as a Daniel Lovelace ballad. It's one of his Christmas originals from an album that came out nine or ten years ago. I used to play his songs on repeat when I was a teenager—drawn to the rasp in his throat, the way he bent notes. This one especially.

I start singing. The bar quiets—people actually stop talking to listen. It's that kind of song. Quiet, aching. About missing home and not knowing where home is anymore.

Halfway through the first verse, I spot a man sitting alone in the back corner. Cowboy hat tipped low over his face, nursing a beer. He's very still.

During the chorus, he sits up straighter. I can't see his eyes under the hat brim, but I feel him watching.

Then suddenly he's standing. Moving fast toward the exit. He knocks into someone's table in his hurry, doesn't stop to apologize, just pushes out into the night.

He leaves so abruptly I wonder if he's having a medical emergency. I almost stop singing to check on him. But no one else seems concerned, so I push the worry aside and finish the song.

The applause is generous. Griselda whistles. I wave and scan the room.

Ivy's pulling on her coat. I start toward her, but then I see my mom at the bar.

She's pale. Her hands grip the edge of the counter, knuckles white. She looks like she's seen a ghost.

I change course, immediately worried. "Mom? Are you okay?"

"I'm fine." Her voice is barely audible. "You sang that beautifully, sweetheart."

"Do you know the song?"

"No. Why would I?" But she won't look at me. "I think I need some air."

She's out the door before I can offer to go with her.

I look around for Ivy, but her table is empty. She left without saying goodbye.

Frustrated, I push through the crowd and leave the restaurant. Outside, I find Mom standing alone, arms wrapped around herself, staring up at the falling snow. She looks small. Vulnerable.

"Talk to me," I say quietly.

"There's nothing to talk about."

"Mom."

She finally looks at me. Her mascara's smudged. "That man. The one in the hat. Did you see him leave?"

"Yeah. During my song. Why?"

"I thought—" She shakes her head. "Never mind. It's impossible."

"What is?"

"Nothing." Her voice breaks. "It's late. I'm tired. Can you take me home? "

"Of course."

We start walking in silence to Ivy's car. I want to push, to ask what's wrong, but she looks so fragile. Like she might shatter if I press too hard.

My phone buzzes. It's Ivy.

"Ivy," I say, relieved.

"Hi. Merry and I brought your mom's bag over to the cottage. I'm going to stay at the loft tonight instead of her."

The words come out rushed, like she's trying to get through them quickly.

"Ivy—"

"You two clearly have a lot of catching up to do. And I'm exhausted. Besides, Holly and Jack want to clean the loft more thoroughly for your mom because Holly is a certified neat freak."

I lower my voice, turning slightly away from Mom. "I'm sorry I didn't get to spend any time with you tonight."

"It's okay. Really. It's only one night. Are we still on for the gingerbread contest tomorrow at Quinn's barn?"

"One hundred percent. I wouldn't miss it."

"Good night, Dash."

She ends the call. I pocket my phone and turn back to Mom. She's watching me with an expression I can't read. It's not worry. Honestly, it looks like satisfaction, but that can't be it.

"Change of plans," I tell her. "You'll stay at the cottage with me tonight."

"Are you sure? I don't want to—"

"I'm sure." Ivy is, at least.

By the time I park Ivy's car in the garage and get my mom settled in at the cottage, I'm exhausted and confused.

Mom being here should be a good thing. We're finally going to have a real Christmas together. But I don't like the growing distance between me and Ivy.

Mom appears in the bedroom doorway. "The bathroom's all yours."

I brush my teeth and splash some water on my face. When I step into the bedroom to say goodnight, my mother hugs me tightly.

"I love you, sweetheart," she says. "You know that, right? Everything I do is because I love you."

"I know, Mom. I love you, too."

As I head to the couch, her words echo in my mind.

Why do they sound like an apology?

CHAPTER 23

A VERY JOLLY PEP TALK

Ivy

I'm nursing my second cup of terrible coffee when I hear the key turn in the lock. I don't even bother looking up from where I'm curled on Holly's pristine white couch, wrapped in a cream-colored throw blanket. The only splashes of color in this place are the painting Jack gave her for Christmas last year and the books on her groaning bookshelves.

"Oh good, you're awake and miserable," Merry announces, sweeping in with Holly right behind her. "We brought reinforcements."

She holds up a bakery box emblazoned with her logo, Sweet Merry's. It probably contains enough calories to sustain an Olympic swim team, if I know her.

"I'm not hungry," I mutter.

"Well, you probably want something sweet anyway. I know Holly doesn't keep sugar in the house." Merry sets the box on the coffee table. "Because she's a psychopath."

Holly breezes past us into the kitchen, already arranging mugs. "Sugar would mask the intense, rich flavor of my coffee."

"Your coffee tastes like regret," Merry calls after her. "Because you take it black and bitter, like your heart."

Despite my mood, I snort. Holly appears in the doorway holding a small basket. She sets it in front of me with exaggerated ceremony.

"I keep creamer and sugar on hand for Jack. Because unlike some people, I'm thoughtful about my partner's needs."

The pointed look she gives me is impossible to miss.

"Subtle," I tell her.

"I'm done with subtle. Subtle went out the window at midnight when you texted to let us know you were sleeping here instead of at the cottage with Dash. You're lucky I have so many spare keys."

Merry claims the armchair and pulls an enormous frosted cinnamon roll from the box. "So. Post-mortem time. How bad was it?"

I dump an unseemly amount of cream into my coffee and watch it swirl. Then I spoon in plenty of sugar. "It wasn't bad. You saw her at karaoke. Rachel was charming. Everyone loved her."

"She was. So why is she at the cottage while you're

moping around my loft?" Holly settles onto the other end of the couch, tucking her long legs beneath her.

"I haven't had a moment alone with Dash since she got here. She dragged him off for a tour of the town, just the two of them. And then, at karaoke, every time we tried to talk, she needed him for something." I take a cautious sip from my mug. Holly's coffee is infinitely better now that it's been doctored. "And then I left without saying goodbye because I felt like I was in the way."

"In the way of what?" Merry asks. "Your own boyfriend?"

"He's not officially my boyfriend," I correct. Then I pause. Or is he? My sisters snort in unison. "Or even if he is, I feel like I'm encroaching on their time together. She came all this way. She's his mother. Of course he wants to spend time with her."

Holly and Merry exchange a look.

"What?" I demand.

"Nothing," Holly says, too innocently. "Except she didn't just show up here. *You* invited her, and now you're mad that she came."

"I'm not mad—"

"You're moping in my loft at eight in the morning, drinking coffee you lack the palate to appreciate, and radiating misery," Holly interrupts. "That's the Ivy version of mad."

I pull the blanket tighter around my shoulders. "I thought I was doing something nice. Giving him a real family Christmas. But now she's here and I feel like ... like I don't belong."

"Did she make you feel that way?" Merry asks carefully. "Or did you make yourself feel that way?"

I open my mouth to answer, then close it. Because the truth is, Rachel didn't do anything overtly wrong. She was polite. Grateful, even, for being invited. So what's my problem?

"It's just a vibe," I say finally. "I'm probably being paranoid."

"Or," Merry says slowly, "this woman you don't really know is suddenly very present in your brand-new relationship. You're allowed to feel weird about that."

Holly nods. "Even if she's lovely. Even if she's his mother. You're allowed to feel what you feel."

"But I'm the one who brought her here!" The words burst out of me, louder than I intended. "Like you said, I called her. And now I'm sitting here feeling sorry for myself because she's actually spending time with her son—which was the whole point of inviting her."

"Two things can be true," she says simply. "You can do a kind thing and still feel uncomfortable with the result."

I slump back against the couch cushions. "I just thought ... I don't know what I thought. That she'd be here and we'd all have this perfect Hallmark Christmas together."

"Life's not a Hallmark movie, Ivy," Merry says gently. "Real relationships are messy. Real families are complicated. You invited his mother to town after fake dating him for less than a week."

"Well, when you put it that way …."

"It's bizarre, actually."

"I know."

"Like, genuinely unhinged behavior."

"I know!"

"We love you," Holly adds quickly, "but this whole idea is completely out of character for you. We're just trying to understand."

I grab a marshmallow brownie from the box, mostly so I have something to do with my hands. "He told me they never had a real Christmas. That it was always just the two of them, working. That she sacrificed everything for his career. I wanted to give him something special."

"That's sweet," Merry says. "It's also a lot of pressure to put on a new relationship—real or fake."

"And on yourself," Holly adds. "You're trying to be the perfect partner who does the perfect thing. But maybe what he needs isn't perfect. Maybe what he needs is for you to be honest about how you feel."

"I can't tell him I'm uncomfortable with his mother being here. I invited her!"

"You can tell him you miss him," Holly counters. "That you want to spend time with him. That you feel like you're on the outside looking in."

"That makes me sound needy."

"It makes you sound human," Merry says firmly. "Ivy, you've been killing yourself to be considerate. To give them space. To not be in the way. But you're allowed to want to be with him."

I take a bite of gooey brownie goodness and chew slowly. "I'm not sure she likes me."

"Did she say something?" Holly's immediately on alert.

"Not directly. But there was this moment when she asked if I really thought Dash could be happy here, and I wasn't sure whether she was genuinely asking or implying that he couldn't."

"See, that feels pointed," Merry says.

"Or it could have been a mother making conversation," Holly argues. "Context matters. Tone matters. Was she hostile?"

"No. That's what's making me crazy. She's pleasant and polite but it feels like she's elbowing me out."

Holly sets down her mug. "Okay. Real talk time. What are you actually afraid of?"

The question catches me off guard. I pull my knees up to my chest. "I'm afraid she'll convince him that this—us, this town, this life—isn't real. That it's just a break from his real life."

Merry shakes her head. "That won't happen. Anyone who's seen you two together can tell it's real."

"It started as fake," I remind her.

"And then it became real," she insists. "You told us. The night he shared your bed, when you asked him to stay— that was real. And yesterday when he told you he wanted to stay in town longer, spend more time with you —real. And this morning when you woke up feeling like you'd made a mistake bringing his mother here—also real. It's all real. The good and the uncomfortable."

I press my palms against my eyes. "What do I do?"

"You give them space today," Holly says. "You let them have their time together but you claim your time, too. At the gingerbread contest, you show up as Ivy. Not as his fake girlfriend, the town ambassador, or the perfect hostess. Just you."

"And if his mom tags along?"

"Then she tags along. And you're polite and kind because that's who you are." She reaches over and squeezes my hand. "But you don't disappear. You don't make yourself small. You finally started taking up space. Don't backslide now."

Merry weighs in. "The point is, you can't protect yourself and build something real at the same time. You have to choose."

I stare into my coffee. "What if I choose wrong?"

"Then you learn something. But running away last night? Sleeping here instead of talking to him? That's also a choice. And I don't think it's the one you actually want to make."

She's right. I know she's right. I left without saying goodbye because I was scared. Because watching him with his mother made me feel like an outsider, and instead of staying and claiming my place, I disappeared.

"Plus," Holly adds, "Jack and I are not spending another night on your lumpy mattress so Rachel can stay in the cottage. If she's not sleeping here, we are."

I laugh. "There it is. The real reason you're here."

"I'm a multitasker. I can support you emotionally and simultaneously reclaim my space."

"Not to mention," Merry chimes in, "she refused my very reasonable request that she pay twenty dollars a night in rent. She and Jack are terrible houseguests."

I giggle and Holly scoffs.

Merry stands and brushes crumbs from her lap onto Holly's spotless beige carpet. "Go to the flower shop. Do a few hours of work. Then go pick Dash up and take him to the contest. You need to be seen in public together, anyway."

I look at my sisters with their fierce loyalty and practical wisdom and the tightness in my chest loosens slightly.

"Thank you," I say quietly. "For coming over. For the intervention."

"Intervention sounds harsh. Let's call it a pep talk," Merry suggests.

"A very Jolly pep talk," Holly agrees. "With the ultimate goal of getting your butt out of my loft."

CHAPTER 24

I MET A GIRL

Dash

Twenty-four hours ago, I was waking up with Ivy in my arms, and now I'm engaged in a battle of wills with my mother. Seems impossible. But, it's happening.

The inciting incident? A slice of toasted bread smothered in sugar plum preserves.

"Mmm," Mom moans, dabbing away a glob of jam on her lip. "This bread is delicious. You'll have to take me to the bakery where you got it before we leave town."

I grin over my coffee mug. "Can't."

"Why not?"

"Because I made it."

She shakes her head. "I don't understand."

"I—we baked it. Ivy and I made the dough, let it rise, then baked it in the oven." I hear the pride in my voice, and, for a moment, I almost feel silly. But frost it. I *am* proud. Why not own it?

Mom drops the toast on the kitchen island like it's a black widow spider and not a delicious breakfast treat. "You *made* it?"

"Yes."

"How long did that take?" She crosses her arms over the front of her ice blue silk pajama top.

"All in, four hours. Maybe a bit longer."

"Four hours? Honey, you don't have four hours to devote to making a basic staple that you can pick up at literally any market—or, if you insist, have Rowan bake for you."

"I'm not traveling with my chef, Mom. And I did have time to make it. There was a lot of hands-off time while the dough rose." Why am I defending myself for baking bread? This is wild.

She sips her iced matcha and shakes her head. "Dasher, what are you trying to prove?"

I stare at her for a long moment. "Nothing."

She stares back, then sighs. "Honey, have you forgotten how closely I work with Brody?"

The swift subject change from artisan bread to my manager gives me mental whiplash. "No. What are you talking about?"

"I know this girl isn't really your girlfriend. I was on the strategy call with Lia Campbell's team, and I was looped in when she backed out."

I wince. Of course, she knows—or thinks she does. "It's true that—"

"Don't misunderstand. Tapping Ivy as a replacement was brilliant. Honestly, she's more effective than Lia would have been. And it's working. Your fans are eating it up. And the studios are excited about the redemption arc, eager to sell the fantasy of you in love with a small-town florist who looks like an angel. Lean into it, darling. But don't forget it's an act."

"It's not an act, though." My voice comes out rough, and I shift gears to soften it. "It was at first, but I really fell for her, Mom."

"Dasher, honestly. You've known her for *four* days."

"Five."

"As if that's any better. Ivy's delightful, yes. This town is charming, yes. But this is not your life."

"It could be."

Her tone is gentle when she says, "No, it can't. Brody told me you haven't returned his call about the meetings he's set up for you. You haven't even committed to the audition for the new Lin-Manuel Miranda musical. That's your dream role. You can't throw away everything you've —no, we've—worked so hard to achieve for a girl you just met. I've sacrificed too much." Tears shine in her eyes.

"Don't you mean *I've* sacrificed too much?"

The question trembles on the air between me and my mother, weighty and dangerous. She takes a sharp breath and presses her palms down hard on the kitchen island. Then she lifts her chin and pins me with eyes so similar to mine it's like looking in a mirror.

"You can't begin to imagine how much I've sacrificed." Her voice quavers.

The words slam into my chest. I curl my hands into fists, reflexively. Then relax them. Fist them again. My breathing is ragged. I have to get out of here before I say something I can't take back.

"I need some air." I grab my coat from the hook by the door and storm out of the cottage with no destination in mind.

I follow the hypnotic whine of the wood lathe and end up in Nick's workshop. He must sense me when I come in because there's no way he hears me. But he turns the wood on the machine two more rotations and then shuts off the lathe.

He removes his safety glasses and looks over his shoulder. "Ha. I was hoping you were Noelle with a fresh cup of coffee."

"Sorry to disappoint."

"I'm not disappointed in the least." He smacks his work gloves together, knocking off the wood shavings, then peels off the gloves and places them beside the manger in progress. "Now I have an excuse to take a break. Come on, son. Noelle may not make deliveries, but she always keeps a pot on in the kitchen."

He gives me a casual slap on the back as we walk from

the workshop to the inn. I'm careful not to so much as glance in the direction of the cottage.

Inside, we stomp the snow off our boots, fill two mugs with hot coffee, and go into the family's living room where we settle into chairs across from the Christmas tree—Ivy's tree.

"Where's Noelle?" I ask, thinking we should see if she wants to join us.

"She's out front, taking care of guests. It's her day off from the library, and I told her to go do something fun but she claims making sure people enjoy their stay is fun." He shrugs with a smile. "So, what are you and Ivy up to today?"

"There's a gingerbread house decorating contest at Quinn's event barn later. We signed up to do that."

"Always a good time. And there's stiff competition. Professional judges and everything."

"Professional gingerbread house judges?" This town gets quirkier by the minute.

Nick chuckles. "A baker, a miller, and an artist. They judge on taste, structural integrity, and aesthetics."

"Sounds serious." After a lull, I say, "Did you always live here?"

"The inn?"

"The town."

He snorts and strokes his trim beard. "Nope. I grew up in New Jersey. Mistletoe Mountain wasn't on my radar, let alone in my long-term plans. I got a degree in hospitality management. My plan was to work for several hotel chains, all over the world, get some experience, and then go run my sister's resort on the Jersey seashore."

"So how'd you end up here?"

"The usual way. I met a girl."

"Ivy's mom?"

"Yep. Carol grew up here and never wanted to leave. Ivy's like her that way. And once I met Carol, I never wanted to leave either." He grins into his coffee mug.

I give him a moment to have his memory. Then I clear my throat. "And now?"

He looks up. "Now?"

"Well, you and Noelle don't have to stay here, right? There are libraries and inns all over the place."

"That's true enough. But no place else is Mistletoe Mountain. Noelle moved away for a while—lived in Europe. But once she came back, she came back to stay. This place doesn't get into everybody's blood. Plenty of people leave. But if it *does* get into your blood, you're done for. Look at Jack. He could be on a beach in Florida right now instead of freezing his Christmas bulbs off in Vermont. But he's here."

"Because he met a girl," I muse.

Nick lifts his mug in salute. "Exactly."

CHAPTER 25

SUGAR AND SPICE AND SACRIFICE

Ivy

Properly caffeinated and powered by sugar, I take a quick shower and help myself to a thick fisherman sweater from Holly's perfectly organized closet. Since I'm about half a foot shorter than her, I style it as a dress. Then I jam my feet back into the torture boots, throw on my coat, and run out the door.

It's a short walk to the flower shop, but my bare legs are numb and frozen by the time I get there. I strike gold when I'm rummaging in a drawer for a skein of twine. I'd tossed a pair of black leggings in there forever ago so that I could catch a class at Maple Twist if an unexpected pocket of time ever opened up. That never happened, but I'm thrilled with the find and wriggle out of the boots to put on the leggings under the sweater dress.

I congratulate myself on my fashion resourcefulness while I pack up the day's deliveries. Farah's offered to handle them for me, so I leave the arrangements on the counter along with a note and a generous tip. My customers will tip her, too, but I know how expensive her textbooks are.

I whip through the rest of my work in record time, eager to get to the cottage early enough to have a heart-to-heart with Dash before we have to leave for the MacIntosh Farm. With any luck, Noelle and Dad can show Rachel around the inn while we talk.

While I'm locking the door, I spot a handful of photographers on the corner. So I turn and give them a wave and a friendly smile. In just a few short days, I've become accustomed to their near-omnipresence.

"Ivy, things must be getting serious between you and Dash if his mom's here," Shane calls. "Any comment?"

I widen my grin but say nothing. Dash told me to never say no comment, but to let them speculate. Speculation drives page views, apparently.

With my entourage of cameramen in tow, I hurry down High Street and turn the corner to head to the cottage. I'm actually looking forward to laying everything out with Dash. My sisters are right. I've come this far, I can't shrink back into my shell now.

At the cottage, when I start to tap in the code on the keyless lock, the door swings open.

"Dash?" I call as I step inside.

No answer.

"Dash?"

The bedroom door opens. Rachel walks out, her expression expectant. When she sees me, it falls. "Oh, hi, Ivy. I heard the door. I thought you were Dasher."

"He's not here?"

She shakes her head. "No. He, um, needed some time to himself."

This is a wrinkle. Now what? I check the clock on my phone. If I can track him down quickly, we'll still have time to talk before we need to be at Quinn's. I just need to hand Rachel off to Noelle and Dad.

Before I can suggest a visit to the inn, she ducks back into the bedroom and emerges with her bag and her coat.

"Can you take me to the loft, please?"

I can't exactly tell her no. And, honestly, it solves the problem of finding something for her to do. Maybe she wants to take a nap or check her emails or something. Whatever it is, she's welcome to do it at Holly's place.

"Sure." I find my key ring in the glossy red bowl on the counter and scoop up my keys.

She's silent as she follows me to the car, silent as we zip over to the loft, silent as I park in Holly's reserved spot. I ask her a handful of questions that she manages to answer by nodding or shaking her head and one shrug. I give up, and we climb the stairs to the apartment in silence.

Inside, I spot the bakery box on the coffee table. Surely, a sweet treat will end our extended game of charades.

"Rachel, would you like a pastry or cookie? My sister baked them."

I'm halfway across the room to grab them when she says, "No, thank you. I had some … some … toast." The word *toast* turns into a wail, and she bursts into tears.

Her shoulders shake. She drops her bag on the floor and buries her face in her hands.

I stand, frozen, in the living room for a moment, trying to think of something helpful to say. I land on, "I'm sorry? … About the toast?"

She hiccups and raises her head to stare at me. Then she bursts out laughing.

Great, Dash's mom is having an emotional meltdown and I have no idea where he is.

"Oh, you're funny." She manages a wistful smile.

I am? I have no idea what's funny about this situation.

"Can I get you anything? A glass of water, maybe?" *Or a therapist? A priest? The number for a good boulangerie?*

"Dasher and I had an argument and he left," she says in response.

"Oh. I'm sorry." I hesitate. "Maybe he's at Quinn's already? The gingerbread contest starts soon."

Her face brightens with desperate hope. "Could you take me there? Please?"

I want to say no. I want to find Dash on my own, talk to him privately. But she's looking at me with those dark eyes —Dash's eyes—and I can't refuse.

"Of course."

"Thank you!" She heads for the bathroom, gesturing

toward her red, puffy eyes. "I need to touch up my makeup first. I'll be quick."

While she's gone, I sink onto Holly's white couch and look around the loft. It's beautiful in a sterile, magazine-spread way. Everything is beige and cream and perfectly arranged. No photos of her and Jack. No messy piles of books or coffee mugs left on side tables. Literally anyone could live here.

When Rachel emerges, her energy has shifted. She looks determined. Her expression is pleasant, but her shoulders are back and there's an intensity behind her eyes.

"Ready?" I ask.

"Ready," she replies, then she sweeps past me to the door.

The MacIntosh Farm barn is aglow with white lights strung across the exposed beams. A dozen large wreaths hang around the barn—three on each wall. I made them from fragrant white pine and sugared cranberries. Their aroma complements the scents of gingerbread, peppermint, and vanilla that waft through the warm barn. Four rows of tables covered with red and white striped table-cloths stand ready for action, holding the necessary components to create a gingerbread masterpiece.

Dash isn't here.

I scan the barn again, hoping I missed him somehow. But no—he's not here.

Beside me, Rachel's shoulders slump as she realizes the same thing.

Then I spot the photographers near the entrance, cameras at the ready, and my heart thumps.

"If he stands you up, it looks bad," Rachel murmurs, giving voice to my exact thought.

Our eyes meet and we wordlessly agree to protect the public narrative we've both helped create.

"We could say we planned to partner together," I suggest. "The two most important women in Dash's life want a chance to get to know each other."

"That's perfect." Relief floods her face.

We claim the last empty table just as Quinn rings the cowbell to start. Around us, teams spring into action—sorting candy, piping icing, fitting gingerbread walls together. The room buzzes with excited chatter and laughter.

Rachel and I work in awkward silence at first. I pipe a careful line of white icing along one wall edge while she holds two gingerbread pieces steady. We're building a small cottage—nothing elaborate. Just a simple house with a peaked roof and a red candy door.

"You're good at this," she says, watching me create scalloped shingles with green icing.

"I like detail work." I hand her a bowl of mini marshmallows. "These can be snow on the roof."

She presses them carefully into place, one by one. Her hands are shaking slightly.

"Ivy," she says after a long pause. "Can I be honest with you?"

My stomach tightens. "Of course."

"You seem like a lovely person. And I can see why Dasher is drawn to you and to this town, this life. It's charming." She adds a peppermint to the path leading to our door. "But he has a life in Los Angeles. A career he's worked toward since he was six years old."

I focus on piping white icicles along the roof edge. "I know, Rachel."

"Do you?" Her voice is gentle but urgent. "There's a role —the lead in the new Lin-Manuel Miranda musical. It's Dasher's dream. The audition is next week and he won't commit to it. Because of you."

The icicle I'm piping goes crooked. I set down the piping bag.

"I didn't ask him to give up his career."

"Maybe not intentionally." She places a gumdrop window with precision. "But staying here means walking away from opportunities. From everything we've—everything he's—worked for."

"I don't want that." I force the words past the hard lump in my throat.

"I know it's hard to think about letting him go." Her hand covers mine briefly. "Especially given your ... situation. Believe me, I know better than anyone."

My situation? I have no idea what she means, but the sympathy in her eyes makes my chest ache. Maybe them spending Christmas here is a bigger deal than I realize?

"Did you?" I ask quietly. "Let someone go?"

She swallows. "Dash's father. I was young—younger than you. I loved him." She places a chocolate kiss on our chimney. "But he had dreams. And I was pregnant with Dasher. I had to choose what was best for him and best for me and the baby, not what I wanted."

"Do you regret it?"

"I still love him," she says simply. "But he got to pursue his dreams. And I got Dasher." She looks at me. "That's what real love is, Ivy. Wanting what's best for someone, even when it breaks your heart."

Around us, teams are laughing, showing off their creations. Cameras flash as photographers capture the festive chaos. Rachel and I smile for them, two happy women decorating a gingerbread cottage. Meanwhile my world crumbles.

We finish in silence. Our cottage is sweet and simple—a red door, marshmallow snow, a chocolate kiss chimney. It looks like a home filled with love.

CHAPTER 26

ON DASHER AND DANCER AND HEARTBREAK

Ivy

In a stroke of miserable luck, Rachel and I win the contest and have to paste on even more frozen smiles as we accept our prize—an intricate Croquembouche tree handmade by Merry, the cream puffs held in place with spun sugar. We beg off the interview request, citing our need to get ready for the Santa Paws event tonight.

I drive Rachel back to the loft on autopilot, then drop the puff pastry tower off in Noelle and Dad's kitchen. I know the guests will gush over Merry's artistry. Someone should enjoy it, and I have no appetite.

My mood doesn't improve when I return to an empty cottage. Dash has come and gone. The still-damp towel hanging on the towel bar in the bathroom and the distinct scent of cinnamon, juniper, and faint musk are dead-give-aways. I blow out a breath and pull out my phone to text him. I nearly drop it when I see I have a text from him. He must've sent it while I was driving back from Quinn's:

> Sorry I missed the contest. Saw you and Mom knocked it out of the park! I headed to the Cat Cafe to do a last-minute walk-through. Your dad left you something to wear tonight. It's in the closet. See you soon.

My dad? This I have to see. I might let Luna dress me, but I draw the line at Nick Jolly as a stylist.

I open the walk-in closet and spot the dress instantly. I cover my mouth with my hand. My parents played Mr. and Mrs. Claus twice a year. In July, my mom wore a vintage cocktail dress, which she left to Noelle. In December, she wore this.

I reach out to touch the sleeve. It's another vintage number. Red velvet with long sleeves. It's off the shoulder, and the top, cuffs, and hemline are all trimmed with white faux fur. Mom's favorite thing about it was the pockets. Noelle wore it the first Christmas for all of ten minutes before declaring that perimenopause is no time to wear velvet and fur. So it's been tucked away ever since. My heart lifts, and then breaks. I've dreamed of wearing this since I was a little girl. I never thought I'd do it while playing missus to a Santa I have to send away.

I change into the dress and pair it with the black stiletto

boots that have somehow managed to grow on me. I arrange my hair in an updo with face-framing curls, apply a cherry red lip stain and coat my lashes with waterproof mascara. I give my reflection marching orders: "Keep it together long enough to raise some money for the animal rescue and prove that Dash isn't a felinophobe. Convince him he should go back to LA. Then you can fall apart."

I pick up the strand of chunky cultured pearls I found nestled in one of the dress pockets and fasten the choker around my neck. Then I re-read the note that accompanied it:

Mom would be so proud of you. I love you, Dad

I fold it into careful quarters and tuck it back into the pocket.

Then I square my shoulder, lift my chin, and walk out the door.

When I step inside the cat cafe, there's a literal record scratch.

"Sorry!" Nebula calls. "Dang, Ivy. You look *hot*."

I flush. "Thank you, but I'm not sure that's a good thing for Mrs. Claus."

Dash crosses the room and takes my hands, holding them out while he admires me. "Mr. Claus begs to differ." His smile warms my belly. "You're gorgeous."

"Thanks. You look pretty good yourself."

He's not wearing one of the innumerable Santa suits the Mistletoe Mountain Santa posse swap back and forth.

Instead, he's wearing a tuxedo. A deep red, velvet tux jacket with black lapels, slim-cut black pants, and a black bow tie.

His eyes crinkle with pleasure. "Yeah?"

"You're the sexiest Santa I've ever seen," I say. It's the unvarnished truth.

He spins me in a circle and my dress skirt flares out. Then he reels me into his chest for a moment before dipping me, his strong hand splayed across my back for support. My lips part on their own accord as I gaze up at him. Some distant part of my brain registers the flashbulbs and clicking of shutters as he lowers his mouth to mine. His breath is hot. My pulse is racing.

Loud applause and several wolf whistles pull me out of our private world. The noise breaks the spell on Dash, too, and he lifts me to standing.

Then he bows and smoothly steps into his role. "Welcome to the first ever Santa Paws benefit. Titus' Teahouse and Cat Cafe is proud to partner with Stillwater Animal Rescue to make the holiday special for Mistletoe Mountain's furry friends."

As he greets the crowd, I spot Rachel. She's sitting at a table with Griselda and Marley. She's not looking at her son. She's staring directly at me. I hold her gaze for a moment then turn to look for my family. When I find them, Dad gives me a wide smile. Noelle holds up heart hands, and Jack gives me a dorky thumbs up. My sisters raise their tea cups in my direction, pinky fingers extended like they're a pair of Edwardian ladies. I stifle a giggle.

The next several hours are a blur of auction bids, heartfelt stories about rescued animals, many, many finger sandwiches and petit fours, and too many cups of tea to count. Cats prowl around the party, getting nibbles of salmon mousse and dollops of nondairy whipped cream from delighted guests. At one point, Quinn flashes a flask and I hold out my cup for a discrete splash of whiskey. Holly passes, and Merry merrily informs us she's got her own flask.

DJ Nebula stops the music, and Titus, Henry Stillwater, and Dash walk to the front of the room. Flanked by Titus and Henry and holding a friendly tabby cat named Dancer, Dash announces that the event has raised eighteen thousand dollars for the animal sanctuary and rescue and resulted in eleven adoptions. At the burst of excited applause, Dancer jerks in Dash's arms. I hold my breath, willing him not to drop the cat. Dash cradles the startled tabby like a baby and strokes its face. I exhale. I'm thrilled to see all of the assembled photographers have captured the moment. Mission accomplished.

Actually, this event has accomplished multiple missions—Titus' cafe is going to be all over social media, the Stillwaters have raised a lot of money and found almost a dozen cats and dogs new homes, and Dash has transformed from an allergic cat dodger to a cat lover. I allow myself a swell of gratitude and satisfaction before I ruin it all by remembering I have a mission of my own to carry out.

Dash finds me in the crowd and presses his mouth near my ear. "Wanna sneak out?"

"Yeah." My voice sounds hollow. "Let's do that."

We slip out the kitchen door and walk through the courtyard. A light snow falls. Christmas lights twinkle. Soft music floats out from the teahouse. It should be romantic. It's not.

"How've you been?" Dash laces his fingers through mine as we head toward the cottage. "I feel like we've barely talked since my mom arrived."

"That's because we haven't. She's kept both of us pretty busy."

He flashes a smile. "That's Rachel Pine for you."

"About your mom. I'm sorry if my surprise was too much. I just wanted you to have the Christmas you never had with her."

He stops walking and takes my shoulders. "I was stunned at first. I'll admit it seemed like a lot. But now that I've had some time to get used to the idea, I'm thrilled."

"Really?"

"Really."

"You should know I called her before I asked you to stay in bed with me, and before you decided to extend your visit."

"I figured as much given the timing."

"In retrospect, that's a lot all at once."

"There's nothing wrong with a lot," he tells me.

We reach the cottage and I key in the code. I wait until we're inside to say, "I heard you and your mom had an argument this morning."

A shadow passes over his face. "It happens. That's a

natural consequence of radical honesty. Sometimes people say things you don't like."

He kicks off his shoes and settles on the couch, opening his arms in an invitation. I take off my boots and join him but don't snuggle into his chest, despite how much I want to.

"I'm about to say something neither one of us will like." I force myself to look at him.

"What's that?"

"We have two more days of fake dating. After that, you should go back to Los Angeles, the way you originally planned."

He goes very still. "What?"

"You should take the meetings Brody set up for you. You should *definitely* audition for the musical. This"—I gesture between us— "was supposed to be temporary. We both knew that."

"It was until it wasn't."

"It's fake, Dash. I forgot that and let myself fall for you. But this will never work. And now your mom's here, and reality's setting in."

"She did this, didn't she?"

"I don't know what you mean."

"My mother. I didn't tell you about the musical. So she must have. She told you to back off, didn't she?" he demands roughly.

"She told me how much she loves you. How hard you've worked for everything you've accomplished." My voice cracks. "You should go home."

"Forget what Rachel Pine wants. Is that what you want?" His voice is dangerously quiet.

"Yes."

"Look at me and say it."

I can't. If I look at him, I'll break. "It's what's best."

"If that's what you believe, look at me and tell me to go home, Ivy."

I stand up and put my boots back on. Then with my hand on the doorknob, I turn and meet his dark, pained eyes from across the room.

"Go home, Dash."

I pull the door open, step out in the cold night air, and break apart.

CHAPTER 27

LADIES DANCING AND LORDS A'DRINKING

Dash

I sit slumped on the couch in my red velvet tux and stare at the door, willing Ivy to walk back into the cottage. When there's a sharp rap on the door, my breath catches. Did I do it? Then I hear Nick calling my name and sigh. The universe sent the wrong Jolly.

I trudge across the room and open the door. Nick, Jack, and Titus stand on the porch, wearing expectant expressions.

I don't invite them in. "Do you need something?"

Nick shoulders his way past me and the others follow. Defeated, I close the door and turn to face them.

"Get out of that monkey suit," Jack tells me. "Go put on jeans and a sweater or something."

"Why?" I demand.

"Because Ivy's bawling her eyes out in my kitchen, and Noelle and my daughters told us to leave. I figure you're over here sulking for the same reason she's crying. So let's go have a beer." Nick delivers this rationale in a matter-of-fact tone.

It has the effect of propelling me to my feet. Halfway to the bedroom to change, I turn around. "Wait. Where's my mother?"

"Griselda and Marley spirited her off to the North Pole Social Club so she could see what high society looks like in Mistletoe Mountain's most exclusive members-only club."

"Oh, she'll like that. What does it look like, though?" My curiosity is piqued.

"Like the rest of Mistletoe Mountain, only the music isn't as loud, and you pay a monthly tab instead of paying at every visit," Nick explains.

"How do you become a member?" Jack wonders.

"It's invitation only," Nick says seriously.

Titus rolls his eyes. "The invitation is printed in the monthly *Mistletoe Mountaineer* magazine. And it's free to join. You just have to scan the QR code."

I can't help laughing. "Why bother?"

"So people can say they belong to the town's most exclusive members-only club. Now change, because we're taking to you an actual private club and you're not walking in with us looking like that."

Nobody bothers to tell me the name of this private club

until I'm squeezed into the back seat of Noelle's hatchback, knees near my elbows, and we're rumbling out of town.

"It's not really a private club," Titus begins, his shoulder rubbing against mine. "But Nick belongs to a club that meets there and they have a private room."

Nick and Jack exchange looks in the front seat. My antenna goes up. "Hold on, what kind of club?"

"The Lords of the Mountain," Nick says. "It's a group of motorcycle enthusiasts."

"*You're* in a motorcycle gang?" I sputter.

"It's more of a club," Titus clarifies. "Dancing Ladies is their headquarters."

"Why do I know that name?"

"It's the strip club where Titus bartends," Jack answers.

"They're exotic dancers, not strippers," Nick corrects.

"No." I grip the back of Nick's headrest. "No, no, no. I cannot be photographed visiting a strip club that's frequented by a bike gang. I'm trying to clean up my image, remember?"

"Nobody's going to let photographers through the doors at Dancing Ladies," Titus reassures me.

Brody will kill me. No, he won't have the chance because my mother will kill me and dump my body in a snowbank.

Sweat beads on my upper lip. "Guys, I really appreciate the gesture, but—"

The car erupts with laughter. Nick's cackling and snorting to the point that I'm afraid he's going to drive us into a ditch. Beside me, Titus shakes with laughter. Finally, Jack wipes his eyes and regains the power of speech.

"You should have seen your face," he tells me. "We're not taking you to Dancing Ladies, don't worry."

"We were just having some fun with you, son. We're going to the fishing cabin. There's a case of Frosty in the fridge. We're gonna listen to music and pontificate. Might even play some cards. A very G-rated evening to take your mind off your troubles."

I exhale, relief washing over me, and lean back against the headrest. It hits me that they're not treating me like Dash Pine. They're treating me like any other guy who just had his heart stomped on by a girl in stiletto boots—which is exactly what I am.

Ivy

"I'll be the designated driver. We won't even have to call a Sober Sleigh," Holly cajoles.

"No." My voice is muffled because my head rests on my arms, facedown on the table.

"Remember how you all forced me to go to the Singles Jingle Mingle last year when Jack and I had that blowup?" She tries a new tack.

"Yes," I answer into the table.

"The peppermint espresso martinis, while tasty, didn't

really help. But dancing with my sisters and my friends *did*, Ivy. And we're not even talking about the Mingle. It's just dancing. In the valley. It'll be dead. You'll feel better if we go dancing."

"I don't want to feel better," I wail.

I hear whispering.

Then, "Ivy Victoria Jolly, sit up."

I do. Mainly because I've never heard Noelle use a mom voice before. I wipe my eyes and stare at her.

She rubs my shoulder. "Go wash your face. Put on your favorite pair of jeans and a flannel shirt and go with Holly and Merry to the Stoneridge Saloon and get your two-step on. Or go to Finnegan's Pub and jig your troubles away."

I purse my lips and consider. "I'll go out on two conditions. One, we go to 80s Night at Sk8phoria Roller Rink. And two, you come with us."

Noelle's face drains of color. "You want me to go roller skating with you?"

Merry's clapping. "It's more like roller dancing, Noelle."

"Especially on 80s night. Or at least that was the case fifteen years ago, which is the last time I set foot in Sk8phoria," Holly chimes in.

After a moment, Noelle pushes herself up from the table. "I guess I better dig out my off-the-shoulder sweat-shirt and leg warmers."

We follow her down the hall and stop at our old bedrooms to forage through storage trunks for vintage neon pink and green sweaters and acid-washed jeans. I know a night of gliding around the roller rink to cheesy hits from the 80s isn't going to change anything. But it'll take my mind off the rock lodged in my chest where my heart should be, and that's better than nothing.

CHAPTER 28

A VISIT FROM VLAD

Dash

I wake up with a pounding headache and a mouth that tastes like I licked the bottom of a fishing cooler. Which, given last night's activities, isn't entirely out of the question.

Fragmented memories surface: Nick dealing cards. Titus telling stories about Dancing Ladies that I'm ninety percent sure were completely fabricated. Jack teaching me some complicated fishing knot that I'll never remember. And beer. So much beer.

I sit up slowly, testing whether my skull is going to split open. It holds. Barely.

The bedroom is flooded with pale morning light. I'm still wearing yesterday's jeans and sweater, minus my shoes. There's a vague memory of Titus and Jack half-carrying, half-dragging me through the front door of the cottage and dumping me on the bed while Nick called out helpful instructions like "don't let him hit his head" and "make sure he's on his side in case he pukes."

I didn't puke. Small victories.

I shuffle to the bathroom, splash cold water on my face, and avoid looking at my reflection. Then I make my way to the kitchen, drawn by the desperate need for something— anything—to make me feel human again.

My travel blender sits on the counter, exactly where I left it. I pull ingredients from the fridge for my hangover smoothie on autopilot: spinach, kale, frozen mango, almond milk, matcha powder. No wheatgrass in this one, but the secret ingredient: a shot of hot sauce. The routine is soothing.

As I'm setting the blender pitcher on the base, I spot the folded piece of paper on the counter, one corner sticking out from underneath the base.

I slide it out and unfold it. It's a note in Ivy's neat, precise handwriting, the letters slightly rounded.

Dash—

I'm at the flower shop. I have a delivery to the children's hospital in the valley this morning. Good PR for you, and it would mean a lot to the kids if you came along. Meet me at Blooms by ten if you want to go.

—Ivy

I read it three times, searching for subtext. The tone is friendly but careful. Professional. Like we're business partners, not whatever we were before I ruined everything.

No. Before she ruined everything. Or before my mother ruined everything?

Before everything was ruined.

I lean against the counter, thinking. She must have come back last night and slept on the couch. Must have woken up early and left before I stirred. I feel a pang of guilt imagining her sleeping in the living room while I was sprawled across the bed, dead to the world.

I fill the pitcher with ice and dump in the ingredients. Press the button, and the blender whirs to life. I drink my green hangover cure standing at the counter, barely tasting it. My phone says it's just past nine. If I hurry, I can catch her before she leaves.

I shower in record time, throw on clean clothes, and I'm out the door in under fifteen minutes.

The walk to Blooms takes seven minutes. The photographers are already stationed outside the shop. They perk up when they see me approaching.

"Dash! Any comment on your mother's visit?"

"What does your mom think of Ivy?"

"What's next for you after Mistletoe Mountain?"

I give them the practiced smile and the casual wave, and push through the door without answering.

Inside, Ivy's behind the counter, wrapping a massive arrangement of red and white flowers in cellophane. She looks up when the bell chimes, and for a split second, her face contorts in—relief? pain? hope?—before she smooths it into a pleasant smile.

"Hi. You got my note."

"I did. Thanks for the invitation." I shove my hands in my pockets to keep from reaching for her. "How are you?"

"I'm fine." The lie is so obvious it hurts. "You?"

"Great. Totally great." Another lie. We're both terrible at this.

She secures the cellophane with a ribbon. "I just need to load these into the car. There are three more arrangements in the cooler."

"I'll get them."

We work in silence, carrying the flowers out to her ancient station wagon. The photographers get their shots —me opening the back hatch, Ivy handing me arrangements, both of us moving with the practiced ease of people who've done this dozens of times.

When the last arrangement is secure, Ivy turns to close the hatch and I'm standing too close. For a moment, neither of us moves.

Then she reaches up and cups my cheek with her cold hand.

The touch is torture. I want to lean into it, to pull her against me, to tell her we're being idiots and we should fix this. Instead, I place my hand over hers on my face for just a second before she pulls away.

"Ready?" Her voice is rough.

"Yeah."

The photographers get this shot, too.

The drive to the valley takes forty minutes. We make small talk for the first ten—the weather, the success of Santa Paws, whether Dancer the cat has been adopted yet. Safe topics that don't require us to acknowledge the enormous thing sitting between us in the car.

Then a song comes on the radio. Acoustic guitar, a raspy voice, lyrics about home and longing and not knowing where you belong.

Daniel Lovelace.

Ivy's hands tighten on the steering wheel. She shifts in her seat, glances at the radio, then at me, then back at the road.

"Are you okay?" I ask.

"Fine. I'm fine." She's not fine. She's agitated, restless, like she wants to climb out of her own skin.

"Ivy—"

"Actually." She cuts me off, her voice too bright. "Would you mind handling the hospital visit yourself?"

I blink. "What?"

"There's something I need to do. It just occurred to me. But the kids—they'll be so excited to see you. You don't need me there. I'm just the flower lady."

"I thought we were doing this together."

"We were. We are." She pulls her bottom lip between her teeth. "There's something I need to take care of. It's important. Can you handle this on your own? Please?"

The song plays on, filling the silence while I try to figure out what's happening. She's lying. Or not lying, exactly, but not telling me the whole truth.

"Sure," I finally say. "I can handle it."

"Thank you." The relief in her voice is palpable. "The hospital staff is expecting us. Well, me. Just tell them you're with Blooms. They'll help you bring everything inside."

She careens into the hospital parking lot, navigates to the main entrance, and puts the car in park but leaves it running.

"You're not even coming inside?" I ask.

"I really need to go. I'm sorry. I'll text you when I'm done and then I'll be back to pick you up."

I climb out, still confused, and she pops the rear hatch.

Before I close the door, I try one more time. "Ivy, what's going on?"

"Nothing. Everything's fine. I just—I'll explain later, okay?"

Her hands are shaking on the steering wheel. Something important is happening. And she won't talk to me.

"Okay," I say, even though it's very much not okay.

I unload the flowers and she gives me one more apologetic look. Then she pulls away from the curb, leaving me standing in the passenger loading zone with no idea what just happened.

Two orderlies push through the automatic doors, both grinning.

"You're Dash Pine!" the younger one says. "Ivy said she couldn't make any promises, but looks like she delivered.

You'll visit with the kids?"

"Yeah. I have the flowers arrangements, too."

"Awesome. The kids are going to lose their minds."

"This is so cool of you, man," the older orderly says, carefully lifting an arrangement and placing it on a dolly. "It's hard for these kids to be cooped up in here during the holidays. We try to make it as fun as we can for them. A visit from Vlad is next level."

I walk in with them as they wheel the flowers inside, smiling and nodding and making appropriate responses. But my mind is elsewhere.

On Ivy, driving away. On the look in her eyes—like she'd just figured something out and couldn't wait another second to act on it. What does she need to do that's so urgent she couldn't even come inside?

I can't answer this question, so I do the only thing I can do: tuck it away and turn to the orderlies. "I could do a storytime for the little ones. Do you happen to have a copy of *And Tango Makes Three* around here?"

CHAPTER 29

AN AMBUSH BY IVY

Ivy

I know I should pull over and calm down. But I don't. Instead, as the last notes of Daniel Lovelace's Christmas ballad fade, I punch Griselda's number into my phone.

She picks up on the second ring.

I skip the niceties. "Where is he?"

"Where is who?"

"You know who."

"For the sake of argument, pretend I don't," she says.

I pound the steering wheel in frustration. "Daniel Lovelace."

There's a pause. Then Griselda says carefully, "Ivy, what are you doing?"

"I'm fixing this. Where is he?"

"Does Dash know you're—"

"Griselda, please. Just tell me where he is. I know you know."

Another pause. I can practically hear her weighing whether to help me or talk me out of whatever I'm planning.

"He's staying at the Stonebridge Tavern in the valley," she finally says.

"Room number?"

"You can't just show up and—"

"What's his room number? Please."

"Ivy." Her voice is firm now. "Think about what you're doing. This isn't your mess to fix."

"Yes, it is."

"Oh, honey." her tone softens. "You're sure about this?"

"I'm sure."

"Okay. He's in Room 412."

"Thanks. Can you do something else for me?"

"Depends what it is."

"Can you pick Dash up at the Children's Hospital and take him and Rachel to the matinee of *The Nutcracker?* I have three tickets at Will Call, but I'm not sure I'll be back in time."

"Well, I *do* love our youth ballet."

This is news to me. She's been feuding with their artistic director for a decade, easy. But I let it go. "Great. I got the best seats in the house, so you should have a fantastic time."

I end the call and type the hotel's address into my GPS system to pull up directions. It's only twenty minutes to the south. I adjust course and turn off the radio so I can think. I need to get Daniel Lovelace to talk to me, trust me, and then do what I want him to do. How hard can it be?

I giggle nervously. Regardless of my likelihood of success, which, frankly, I estimate as low, I've at least broken my habit of shying away from risk.

The Stonebridge Tavern's been around almost as long as the country has, and it looks its age. Once a way-stop for weary travelers, it now serves mainly as overflow accommodations for visitors to Mistletoe Mountain's holiday celebrations who can't find lodging in town. Dad's been known to direct tourists to this place when the inn's completely booked.

I park in the visitor lot and sit for a moment, hands gripping the steering wheel, and gather my resolve. Then I force myself out of the station wagon and across the lot to the hotel. The lobby is clean and bright, but nearly devoid of holiday decorations—at least by Mistletoe Mountain standards. The desk clerk barely looks up as I cross to the elevator. Fourth floor. Room 412.

I'm about to knock on a stranger's door and blow up his world. Except he doesn't feel like a stranger. Not really. I've been listening to his voice all week without knowing it. Every time Dash laughs, every time his speaking voice drops into that raspy register, I've been hearing echoes of Daniel Lovelace.

I knock before I can overthink it.

Footsteps. Then the door opens.

Daniel Lovelace is built like Dash, with the same height and the same broad shoulders. He's older, of course. Weathered. He wears jeans and a faded tour t-shirt and his feet are bare. And when he looks at me, I see Dash's eyes. Dark brown, deep, intense.

"Can I help you?" His famous voice is careful, guarded.

"I'm Ivy Jolly." The words come out steadier than I feel.

"I know who you are." Of course he does. Anyone with a pulse and an internet connection probably knows who I am now. The weirdness of this fact almost knocks me off course.

I refocus. "I want to talk to you about Dash."

His expression shifts, opening up like he's been waiting for this conversation.

He steps back, opening the door wider. "Come on in."

The room is neat but lived-in. A guitar case sits propped against the wall. On the desk, a notebook lies open to a page covered in scratched out lyrics. Half-empty coffee cups litter the nightstand and the dresser.

He gestures to the armchair by the window. I sit. He sits across from me and kicks his long legs out. The posture pings something in my memory.

"You were at Christmas karaoke. You sat in the back and had a cowboy hat pulled down over your eyes."

"Yup."

He's the man who left in a hurry when Dash sang the Daniel Lovelace song.

"How long have you known you're his father?" I ask.

"Since I broke my leg on tour two years ago. Or at least, I suspected then. I was laid up in Albuquerque and an episode of the vampire football series came on. I'd never seen it, and I didn't have anything better to do. Ended up binge watching all seven seasons."He chuckles.

"It sucks you in," I agree, smiling a little at my unintentional pun.

He nods and goes on. "The kid who played Vlad sure reminded me of myself. I started to wonder. Pine's not the most common surname, and I'd had a romance with a girl with that last name."

Daniel stands and moves to the window, staring out at the parking lot.

"Once I was up and around again, I dismissed it. Then I saw his new movie, the one about the rancher. I spent the whole film trying to remember to breathe. It was like watching myself at twenty-five. The same face. The same mannerisms. And now that he's grown, the same voice."

His voice is raw, anguished. So I wait a beat, giving him time.

"But you didn't reach out to him?"

"What was I supposed to say? Hi, I'm the father who never knew you existed. The one who chased record deals and played dive bars while your mother raised you all alone."

He has a point. "But why not contact his mother?"

"Rachel and I were together in the late nineties. I was nobody, playing opener slots for fifty bucks a night. She was trying to make it as an actor, auditioning for commercials, sit-coms, anything. We were young, broke, and stupid. And completely in love." He pauses. "At least I was. Then one day she was gone with no explanation. She just vanished."

"And you let her?"

He spreads his palms wide. "What could I do? She wouldn't return my calls, my letters came back undelivered. I went to her apartment, but she'd moved out. I thought"—he stops and then restarts—"I thought she decided I wasn't ever going to make it and she was tired of waiting. At some point you have to stop the chase."

"But twenty-some years later, you couldn't call her and ask her if Dash was your son?"

Daniel closes his eyes. "She obviously didn't want me in his life. And … I still love her. I've never stopped. Crazy as that sounds. I couldn't risk contacting her and hearing she'd moved on. I'm not proud of it, but it's true."

My chest tightens. There's more to this story, I'm sure of it. But that's not why I'm here.

"The plan," I say. "The whole scheme with Lia Campbell, revealing their fake relationship in Mistletoe Mountain—you were behind that, weren't you?"

He opens his eyes, startled. Then he laughs dryly. "After Dash had that meltdown on the morning show I had to do something. I've been there, spiraling in the spotlight. So I reached out to an old friend."

"Griselda?"

He nods. "She was a dancer on one of my first stadium tours. We've stayed in touch, and I know she's savvy. She knows a lot about reputation management. She put me in touch with Lia Campbell's team. I put a bug in their ear, and they went for it. I also suggested the town where Griselda lived as the perfect place to go public. Figured I'd come up and watch him right his ship."

"Fathering from a distance."

"Better than nothing."

"Is it, though?" The words come out sharper than I intend. "Because right now, Dash is at a children's hospital playing Vlad the vampire for sick kids, trying to be everything to everyone, and he doesn't know the one thing that might actually help him understand himself."

"What's that?"

"That he comes from someone who understands longing. Who turned loss into art. Who knows what it's like to live in the public eye."

Daniel's jaw works. "You think telling him will help?"

"I think he deserves to know his father didn't abandon him."

Daniel's eyes are bright and damp.

"Rachel's here," I continue. "In Mistletoe Mountain. She and Dash are barely speaking. She's trying to protect him by taking away his agency. She's repeating history."

"What do you mean?"

"She told me"—my voice cracks—"real love is letting someone go to pursue their dream. She said she knows it's hard because she did it herself. She said she loved Dash's father but she let him go to pursue his dreams."

"What if they don't want to see me?"

"What if they do?"

He's quiet for a long moment. Then he says, "Why do you care so much?"

"I love Dash." The words are out before I can stop them. "I've only known him for six days, but I love him. And even though I screwed everything up between us by pushing him away, I want him to have just *one* family Christmas, for fig's sake."

He holds my gaze. "Okay. Let's make it happen." Then, "Did you just say for fig's sake?"

The drive back to Mistletoe Mountain takes forever and no time at all. I call Griselda, who confirms she picked up Dash. She asks if I found Daniel. I say yes. She asks if I know what I'm doing. I say no, but I'm doing it anyway.

"That's the way," she says with a smile in her voice.

I hang up and turn the radio on. A Daniel Lovelace song is playing. Of course it is.

As he sings about finding his way back home, I realize that all these songs about love, loss, and yearning are really about Rachel.

CHAPTER 30

THREE THINGS

Ivy

I must've set tables for hundreds of events at the inn. Wedding receptions. Anniversary dinners. Holiday parties where families who actually like each other gather to celebrate.

This is nothing like any of those.

"Are you sure about this?" Noelle asks, smoothing the tablecloth for the third time.

"No," I admit, arranging silverware with trembling hands. "But I can't think of another way."

The dining room looks beautiful, at least. All the food is laid out on platters in the middle of the table. Family-style, the way we do Sunday dinners. Roast chicken, roasted vegetables, and fresh bread, still warm, courtesy of Merry.

It's all comfort food, because something tells me we're going to need comfort tonight.

I count the place settings to make sure there are nine: Dash, me, Rachel, Daniel, Dad, Noelle, Merry, Holly, Jack.

"What if this blows up in my face?" I adjust a water glass that doesn't need adjusting.

"Then it blows up," Noelle says. "But at least you'll know you tried."

Dad appears in the doorway. "Ivy, are you sure you don't want to let Dash know Daniel's coming, and who he is?"

"Even if I wanted to, it's too late now." My stomach twists.

"This seems risky," Dad said carefully.

"I know." I set down the glass before I break it. "But he's been with his mom all day. If I told him, he'd confront her. I think that would go sideways and they wouldn't show up at all. This way, all three of them are here. There's at least a chance that they'll face things head on."

"I hope you know what you're doing, sweetpea."

"Me, too, Dad." I straighten a napkin. "But Daniel deserves to meet his son. Dash deserves to know his father. And Rachel"—I pause—"deserves a chance to stop running."

The kitchen door opens. My heart stops.

"That's Daniel," I say quietly. "I'll get him."

I walk into the kitchen. Daniel hovers in the doorway.

"Griselda told me to come in this way. I hope that's okay." His voice is strained. He's nervous, too.

"This is the family entrance," I confirm. "Come on in."

He steps further into the kitchen. "Are they here?"

"My sister is at the cottage now, getting them. They don't know you're coming," I confess. "Neither of them. I'm sorry to spring you on them like this, but it's the only way."

Daniel's face pales, then he exhales. "I sure hope you know what you're doing, kid."

That makes two of us. Three, actually, because my dad just said the exact same thing.

"The family room is down that hall." I gesture toward it. "Make yourself comfortable. They'll be here soon."

My dad comes around the corner and greets Daniel Lovelace in that warm, friendly innkeeper way of his. As they walk together toward the family room, I look out the window over the sink. Merry is leading Dash and Rachel down the path from the cottage. The fairy lights strung in the trees light their way. A moment later, headlights shine in the dark as Holly turns into the driveway and parks. Jack pops out of the passenger seat to open her door for her. They intercept Merry and the Pines, and they all walk the rest of the way together.

The gang's all here.

I remind myself to breathe.

Dash

*M*om and Holly are keeping up a steady stream of chatter. I'm barely paying attention. Ivy's been avoiding me ever since she bailed on me at the children's hospital. She didn't even show up at *The Nutcracker.* She sent Griselda in her place. Then, out of nowhere, she invites me and Mom to dinner with the entire Jolly family.

I can't figure out what she's up to. And I'm not sure I should care. She wants me to leave town after tomorrow, after all. She's done with us.

Ivy greets us and sends everyone into the dining room. But she catches my hand as I try to walk by with the others. Her skin is like ice.

"Hey," she whispers, her voice shaking. "Before you go in there, I just want to say—I didn't know how else to do this."

"Do what?" I whisper back, but she's already moving toward the dining room.

What did she do?

I follow her through the pocket doors in time to see Mom take in the table, the place settings, and the family-style spread. Then she stops so abruptly I almost walk into her.

A man's entering the room from the Jolly's living room, flanked by Nick and Noelle. Is that … Daniel Lovelace?

"Rachel." His famous rasp is barely a whisper.

Mom stares at him, her face draining of color. "Danny?" her voice breaks.

"It's been a long time." Then he looks at me. "Hi, son."

I look at him, really look at him, and I see my eyes, my cheekbones, my long tapered fingers.

I jerk my head toward Ivy, the question all over my face. She nods, her green eyes bright with unshed tears.

Daniel Lovelace is my father.

The silence stretches. Mom gapes at Daniel from just inside the doorway. Daniel—my father—hasn't moved. The Jollys are shuffling around uncomfortably.

"Dasher, how could you?" Mom's voice is pure betrayal.

"Not me," I say quickly. "I didn't know he'd be here. I didn't even know who he was—is."

She spins to face Ivy. "You did this."

"Yes," Ivy says. "I did."

"You have no right—"

And my frozen astonishment melts as hot anger bubbles up. "She has no right? *You* had no right. You told me you didn't know who my father was. My entire life, I've wondered. And you've known this whole time."

"You don't understand—" she begins.

"I didn't know." Daniel steps forward. "Rachel, I didn't know you were pregnant. You left without telling me."

"You wouldn't have cared," Her voice cracks. "You were about to go on tour, it was your big break. We were so young, and you weren't ready."

"You didn't give me a chance to decide!" Daniel's composure breaks. "I loved you. I would've—"

"You would've what? Given up your dreams? Your

career?" She's crying now. "I wasn't going to let you make that mistake."

"It wasn't your choice to make," I choke out. "You decided for all three of us."

Ivy

Dash and his mom face each other, a lifetime of secrets cracking open between them. Daniel steps forward, then back. He's not sure whether or how to intervene. I know the feeling.

"Dasher, you know that my parents disowned me when they found out I was pregnant." Rachel's voice is raw. "But what you didn't know is that before I told them, I went to your father's house. To talk to him and figure out how to make this—us—work. And *his* mother took one look at me, at my baby bump, and begged me not to ruin his life. She said he had a future ahead of him and if I truly loved him, I wouldn't tie him down."

That sounds familiar.

Daniel's jaw tightens. "My mother knew? And she said that to you?"

"She loved you," Rachel whispers. "She didn't want you to give up your music."

"So the two of you made the choice for me." His face is stricken.

"I was nineteen, pregnant, and terrified," Rachel says. "I

thought I was doing the right thing." Her voice rises, desperate. "Actually, I'm sure I did the right thing because now that history's repeating itself, I truly understand what your mom meant."

Dash shakes his head. "How is history repeating itself?"

Rachel gives me a look, then turns to her son. "Ivy's pregnant."

I stare at her, genuinely confused. "What?" I manage.

"You're pregnant?" Merry squeals.

"I'm not pregnant!" I eye Rachel cautiously. This is even weirder than the toast thing. "What are you talking about?"

"You were drinking herbal tea during karaoke," Rachel says, frantic. "And I saw the prenatal vitamins. In your bathroom."

"I ordered that tea for Holly," I say slowly, trying to figure out what she's talking about. "What vitamins?"

"I saw them with my own eyes, Ivy. In your loft on the bathroom vanity."

"Holly's loft," I correct her. "I don't live there. Merry and I live in Noelle's old place."

"Those are my vitamins," Holly says, her face bright red. "I thought I put them back in the cabinet."

"You're pregnant?" I ask my sister.

"Holly?" Merry's eyes are huge.

"No! I mean, not yet. Jack and I are trying to have a baby, though. We're going to be doing the long-distance thing for who knows how long. And, you know, logistically it'll be complicated … so we're going for it now."

"That's why you haven't been drinking," I say.

"Right."

"You had a beer after the tree lighting, though," Merry says.

"It was nonalcoholic," Jack explains. "We weren't ready to tell anyone yet. Guess that ship's sailed." He laughs.

"You're trying to get pregnant?" Noelle sounds delighted. Dad grins like a fool.

"We just started. Let's all keep our expectations in check," Holly says. But a glimmer of a smile slips through her lawyer mask.

"So you're not pregnant?" Rachel asks me.

"I've known your son for six days," I tell her. I know my face is flaming because my skin is on fire. "We haven't even ... you know. Yet."

During the absolutely mortifying silence that follows, I pray for a hole to open up in the floor and swallow me.

No such luck.

Dad breaks the silence, clearly trying not to laugh. "So to be clear, nobody's pregnant. Except possibly future Holly."

"Nobody's pregnant," I confirm, still blushing furiously.

Rachel sinks into the nearest chair. "I thought—"

"You thought history was repeating itself," Dash says. "But it's not. Because I'm not Dad, and Ivy's not you."

I catch him glancing at Daniel when he says "Dad."

"I'm sorry, Ivy." Rachel's voice is small. "When I noticed you weren't drinking and then saw the vitamins, I panicked. I thought you brought me here to tell me you and Dash were going to make a huge mistake."

"Loving someone isn't a mistake," I say quietly. "Running away from love is."

She flinches like I hit her.

"Why don't we sit?" Dad suggests gently. "The food's getting cold."

Dash

And just like that, we sit down to eat. It seems absurd. After all this trauma and revelation, we're just eating dinner. But maybe that's what families do. They sit together even when everything's broken, because sitting together is how things start to heal.

Daniel—I can't think of him as Dad, not yet—sits across from me. He keeps glancing at me like he's afraid I'll disappear. Mom won't look at anyone. Ivy is next to me, and her hand finds mine under the table.

We eat in silence at first.

"I have an idea," Noelle says suddenly. "Our family has a tradition. Every night at dinner, we share three things. Something we're grateful for. Something we regret. Something we're going to do to make tomorrow better."

"Noelle—" Nick starts.

She looks around the table. "I think it's what we need right now. To say what we're really feeling. Out loud."

Her suggestion is met with more thick, heavy silence.

Then Nick clears his throat. "I'll go first."

He looks at each of us in turn. "I'm grateful we're all here. That nobody walked away, even though it would've been easier."

Mom's shoulders shake.

"I regret that some of you are in pain, now," he continues. "That I can't take that away for you." He looks at Ivy for a long beat.

"Tomorrow," he finishes, "I'm going to keep showing up. For all of you." Then he adds, "And I'm going to finish that elfing manger if it's the last thing I do."

When the laughter dies down, Noelle speaks. "I'm grateful for truth. Even when it hurts. Especially when it hurts, because that means someone was brave enough to have a tough conversation."

Ivy squeezes my hand.

"I regret every time I ever chose fear over honesty."

Nick reaches for her hand.

"Tomorrow, I'm going to take Holly to the library and check out every book about motherhood we have on the shelves."

More laughter. Holly laughs the loudest.

It's Ivy's turn, and my heart is pounding.

"I'm grateful I asked Dash to help me with that heavy planter."

"Asked? More like directed," I tease.

She smiles, then grows serious. "I regret that I thought I could decide what was right for both of us. That was wrong."

"Tomorrow," she continues, "I'm going to wake up in bed next to Dash. I hope."

Her face is beet red again, but she holds her head up. Progress.

It's my turn.

"I'm grateful I finally know the truth about my father." Daniel's eyes meet mine, bright and damp.

"I regret the time we lost. All of us." I look at Mom, then back at Daniel. "Time we can't get back."

Mom makes a small sound.

"But tomorrow"—my voice catches—"after I wake up in bed with Ivy, I'm going to build the life I want. Not the life someone else chose for me."

Mom's face crumples, but she doesn't interrupt.

Daniel goes next. He's been quiet through most of dinner. Now he clears his throat.

"I'm grateful to Ivy," he says. "She's given me a chance to meet my son and to see Rachel again."

Mom's head lifts slightly.

"I regret not coming to find you sooner." His voice breaks. "The first time I saw that Vlad show and I wondered, I should've—"

"You didn't know," I say.

"I should've found out," he insists.

He takes a shaky breath. "Tomorrow, I'm gonna figure out how to be part of your lives. Yours, Dash. And your mom's. If she'll have me."

Holly, Merry, and Jack go next—their three things are

simpler, about family and support and being there for each other.

Then, at last, it's Mom's turn.

She takes a sip of water before speaking.

"I'm grateful for Ivy. For being brave about so many things that I've never been able to be brave about. For leaning into love instead of running away from it."

"I regret"—Mom stops and composes herself—"so much. Not having more faith in Danny. Trying to control Dash's life because I was scared he'd get hurt. And letting that fear hurt Ivy."

She's crying openly now. Holly passes her a napkin.

She looks at me and then at Daniel. "Tomorrow, I'm going to start trying to fix the things I broke."

The silence that follows is different from the earlier ones. Softer. Less jagged.

"Well," Nick says finally. "We should finish eating before the food gets any colder."

"And I made an *amazing* dessert," Merry announces. "If I do say so myself."

"You do," Holly and Ivy tell her in unison.

Scattered laughter breaks the tension. Jack passes the bread. Careful conversations start up.

Nothing's fixed, not even close.

But it's a first step.

CHAPTER 31

WE FINALLY ... YOU KNOW.

Dash

After dinner, I find myself on the porch with Daniel. Neither of us plans it—we just both end up here, needing air, needing space.

"I don't expect anything," he starts.

"I want to know you. I want to hear about your life. Your music. Everything."

"I'd like that." His smile is shaky. "We have a lot of catching up to do."

"Will you stay in town through Christmas?"

"If you want me to."

"I do."

He pulls me into a hug. It's awkward and tentative but,

for the first time in my life, my father puts his arms around me.

After a moment, he clears his throat and slaps me on the back. Then he says, "I've got a question for you."

"Shoot."

"Is your mother dating anyone?"

I blink. Not the question I was expecting. "Uh, no. She doesn't date. Ever."

He gives me a long look. "Would you mind if—?"

"Listen, I think we've all learned not to ask other people's permission to be in love. That's between you and Mom," I say, and I mean it.

He grins. "Fair enough."

Mom finds me later, in the kitchen where I'm helping Ivy wrap up leftovers.

"I don't know how to fix this," she says quietly.

"You start by letting me make my own choices," I say.

"Even if I think they're wrong?"

"Especially then."

She nods slowly. "I'll try. I can't promise I'll be good at it."

"Just try," I say. Then, because she's still my mother, I pull her into a hug. "That's all I ask."

She holds on tight, and I let her.

It's past eleven when Ivy and I finish saying our good-byes and finally leave the inn. We're both quiet during the short walk to the cottage as we process everything that happened.

Inside, I collapse on the couch. Ivy curls up next to me,

and I wrap an arm around her. The closeness feels right after so much distance.

"That was—" I start.

"A lot," she finishes.

"Yeah."

We sit in silence for a moment. Then my phone rings. Brody.

"His timing always did suck," I mutter, but I answer it. "Hey."

"I heard about dinner," Brody says without preamble. "Your mom called me."

"Of course she did."

"She said she was wrong. That I should listen to you. So I'm listening. What do you want?"

I look at Ivy, snuggled into my side, her head on my shoulder.

"I want to take the meetings," I say. "But I'm not going to LA. I'm willing to go to New York to audition for the musical, but anyone else who wants to meet me can come here."

"To Vermont?"

"Yes."

He's silent for a long time. "Aren't you leaving the day after tomorrow?"

I glance at Ivy while I say, "I hope not."

She turns her face up to me and smiles. My heart feels like it might explode. I smooth my hand over her hair and try to concentrate. "Planes fly in both directions, Brody. So set up the meetings but set them up here."

"You're serious."

"I am."

"That's actually not a bad negotiating position," he says slowly, thinking it through. "It shows you have leverage. Gives you power in the relationship."

"So you'll make it happen?"

"I'll make it happen. That's my job. And for what it's worth? I think you're making the right call."

"Why's that?"

"I saw that first fake kiss just like the rest of the world. You were toast from that moment on."

He hangs up laughing.

Ivy pushes herself up to seated. "You're really staying?"

"I'm really staying." I pull her closer. "Is that okay?"

She kisses me instead of answering. It's a heck yeah kind of kiss.

Outside, snow starts to fall again on Mistletoe Mountain. Tomorrow, there will be more conversations to have, more healing to do, more pieces to pick up.

But right now, I'm exactly where I want to be.

Finally.

There's just one more thing I want to do tonight. I swoop her up in my arms and carry her squealing and laughing to the bedroom.

CHAPTER 32

CHRISTMAS MORNING

Two and a half weeks later
Ivy

The morning light filtering through the bedroom windows is soft and golden, catching dust motes in the air like tiny stars. No alarm. No agenda. No photographers—they finally got bored enough or cold enough to leave town.

It's just me and Dash, spooning the way we always do under the thick down comforter, his breathing steady against my hair.

This is peace.

I turn onto my side and trace lazy circles on his chest, thinking about how much has changed in such a short time. Daniel and Rachel have been staying together in

Stonebridge—actually together, like a couple. They're moving fast, but I don't exactly have room to talk. Not when I'm lying here with my fake boyfriend who became very real, very fast.

Dash stirs, his hand sliding up my spine. "Merry Christmas."

"Merry Christmas." I kiss his jaw. "I have something for you."

"Wait."

"Nope. Me first." I scramble out of bed before he can protest and grab the wrapped box from the hiding spot in the closet.

He sits up against the headboard, his thick hair adorably rumpled, watching me with those intense brown eyes that never fail to make my stomach flip. When he tears off the paper, opens the box, and sees the framed photo, his sleepy expression softens. It's a shot of him, Rachel, and Daniel, their arms slung over one another's shoulders, grinning after they've crossed the finish line at the annual Run Rudolph Run 5K.

"I love it." He places it on the nightstand with care.

"You said you don't have any family photos." I settle beside him, shoulder to shoulder. "Now you do."

He doesn't speak. Just pulls me close, his face pressed into my neck. I feel the shudder of his breath and hold him tighter.

After a moment, he clears his throat. "Okay. My turn. But you have to close your eyes."

"Come on."

"Close them," he repeats.

"Okay, but this better not be a matcha wheatgrass latte, Dasher."

He laughs, and I close my eyes, listening to his footsteps leave the room. There's rustling, a soft sound I can't quite place, and then he's back.

"Okay. Open them."

He's holding a small black kitten with huge honey-colored eyes. The cat studies me curiously over a red bowtie.

"Is that King Cole?" I gasp, remembering the cat from Titus' cafe who got Dash into so much trouble.

"Sure is."

"But he's not one of the Stillwater cats. Isn't this Titus' cat?"

"He was a teahouse cat, but he adopted me when Titus and I were doing the Santa Paws planning. If I sat down, he found my lap. If I stood up, he crawled up on my shoulder like a parrot. So, I kept taking the allergy meds to spend some time with him whenever I had a few minutes." He grins. "He's ours. If you want him."

Ours. The word settles in my chest like a promise.

Dash places the kitten on the bed. I let him sniff my fingers and wait until he rubs the side of his face against my palm before I scoop him up. He's purring, a rumbling engine against my chest. "He's perfect. I love him. You."

"I love you, too." Dash climbs back into bed and wraps his arms around both of us—me and our fluffy ball of affection. "Merry Christmas, Ivy."

Later, we'll tromp through the snow for the traditional Jolly family charcuterie board Christmas meal and present exchange before we all help serve Christmas dinner to the inn's guests. Daniel and Rachel are going to join us this year, as my family's circle keeps expanding to make room for more people, more love.

But at this moment, inside the cottage, wrapped in Dash's arms with King Cole purring between us, I'm already home in our circle of three.

Dear Reader,

This book was *supposed* to be a playful holiday romp. And it is—or at least, I hope it is! But it insisted on becoming something in addition to a fake dating/celebrity and girl next door rom-com.

Ivy wanted me to tell a story about making yourself small for so long that you forget who you are. Until one day, you step out of the shadows and stand in the light, vulnerable and unprepared. Dash needed to find family, first through the Jollys, and then by tackling the missing pieces of his biological family and the mess that family can entail. Rachel and Daniel's story is about regret and repair.

And, as always, Mistletoe Mountain is about community, giving and accepting grace and forgiveness, and embracing your sparkle even if everyone else finds it cringe-worthy.

As an added bonus for the author, this is the third book

out of fifty-three that let me get all the way to the end before demanding a full rewrite. But if I've learned anything, it's to trust the process. So, here it is, my rewritten Christmas story, just for you.

Love,
Melissa

Thank you for reading *Booked for Christmas*. If you're new to Mistletoe Mountain, you can read Nick and Noelle's story in *Home for Christmas in July* and Jack and Holly's story in *Booked for Christmas*.

All my books. If you're new to my books, you have a lot of choices! My website melissafmiller.com contains an up-to-date list of *all* my books.

USA Today bestselling author Melissa F. Miller majored in English literature with concentrations in creative writing poetry and medieval literature and was stunned, upon graduation, to learn that there's not a robust job market for such a degree. After working as an editor for several years, she returned to school to earn a law degree.

After practicing law for fifteen years, including a stint as a clerk for a federal judge, nearly a decade as an attorney at major international law firms, and several years running a two-person law firm with her lawyer-husband, she turned in her bar card to make up stories instead.

Now, powered by coffee, she writes full time from the

Pennsylvania home she shares with her family and their cat and dog. (The cat's in charge.)